EXTINCTION HORIZON

C. B. RIPLEY

SEVERED PRESS
HOBART TASMANIA

EXTINCTION HORIZON

For Jeff

ONE

The door slid shut behind Greyson with a solid thump. He slumped back against it, letting out a sigh of relief.

Greyson took a moment to catch his breath and glance around. The comms room looked much the same as it had that morning, when he had brought along a tray of microwave-fresh pastries on his way to the lab. It was a Thursday, so Sophia was on shift. The pretty young technician had gratefully accepted the pastries, though had then claimed to be too busy to chat with him while she ate them. The bitch.

Sure enough, there was the pastry box abandoned on the floor, under Sophia's desk. The corner of a half-eaten bear claw poked out from beneath the cardboard. Of Sophia though, or of her less-attractive colleagues, there was no sign.

He hoped that she was safe. Even though she was a stuck-up tease who didn't know a good thing when it was offered, nobody deserved to die. Not in the ways he'd just seen.

He let out a sob. The last few minutes flashed before his eyes, a kaleidoscope of horror. Panic rose in his chest and took hold of his windpipe. He gasped. He didn't want to die. Not now. Not like that.

Clutching his head in his hands, Greyson took a steadying breath. "Easy," he muttered to himself. "Remember why you're here."

His gaze came to rest on the communications console. It was still lit up, which was a good sign.

Greyson stepped away from the door and took a seat. Even better, it was still logged in to Sophia's account; there wouldn't be any need to try and hack the clearance he'd need to send a message off-station.

A third bit of luck: the emergency broadcast icon was right there on the screen, pulsing scarlet. He'd been afraid the function would be hidden away, costing him valuable time in locating it.

Greyson adjusted the console's camera. He took a moment to compose himself, wiping the sweat from his face and using the dampness to slick back his hair, keeping it from falling into his eyes.

"Okay then," he whispered to himself, finger hanging over the activation icon. "Time to call in the cavalry."

Scratch. Scratch.

He froze. Had he just heard a...

Scratch, scratch, scratch.

There it was again. Right outside the door.

Greyson let out an involuntary whimper then clamped his hands across his mouth to muffle any further sounds.

Something had found him.

Greyson held his breath for what felt like hours. He ignored the pain in his oxygen-starved lungs and listened, straining to hear any further sound.

With a jolt, he realized that he had forgotten to secure the door. The green light above the lock glowed accusingly in the gloom.

He froze, staring at the light, trapped in indecision. He could wait out his pursuer and hope that it couldn't or wouldn't open the door, or get up to lock the door, risking being heard.

The silence stretched out. Greyson heard no more scratching noises. None of the terrible roaring that had echoed around the station halls as his colleagues screamed and died.

Greyson sucked in a breath. His hands were balled into fists and he squeezed them tightly, ragged nails digging into his palms. The pain seemed to calm him, bringing him back to himself.

Moving slowly, afraid to make even the slightest sound, he stood and padded across the room. His stomach roiled as he got closer to the door. Reaching out from as far away as he could, Greyson flicked the lock switch.

The lock light remained green.

Muttering a curse, he flicked the switch again. Nothing happened.

He tried again and again. Still nothing. The door wouldn't lock.

The door wouldn't lock.

He backed away in horror. Frantically, he looked around the room. There were no other ways out. He had trapped himself somewhere that wasn't even secure.

Something slammed into the door.

Greyson screamed, loudly and high-pitched. A hungry snarl came from the other side of the door. He screamed again before shoving a fist into his mouth and biting down on it, hard. Wet warmth ran down his legs.

Another crash came from the door, which began to buckle.

"Oh God," Greyson moaned. He looked around the room wildly, desperate for any escape, but there was nothing. The room was plain and functional. Aside from the comms console and single chair, there was a server stack in one corner and a monitor mounted on one wall. There were no cupboards to hide in, no air vents to crawl through. Even the light was a flat self-luminating panel nested amongst the other ceiling panels, so he couldn't even turn off the lights and hide in darkness.

Wait. Ceiling panels.

Of course! The admin areas didn't have the same secure ceiling structures as the labs. They were just flat polythene panels laid over a metal grid. Strong enough to support his weight but not secured. If he moved one aside, he could climb through the ceiling.

Ignoring the angry growling from the far side of the door, Greyson stood on the chair. He lifted the closest panel and poked his head through into the crawl space. It was dusty but otherwise empty. The perfect escape route.

He was about to pull himself up when he remembered that he hadn't sent out the emergency broadcast yet. He hesitated; this was the only room it could be sent from. If he left without sending it, nobody would know about the attack. Rescue wouldn't be coming.

With one eye on the door, Greyson climbed back down into the room. He pressed the emergency broadcast icon. The console pinged, letting him know that it was ready to record his broadcast. With an effort of will, he shut out the sounds of crashing and snarling, and began to speak.

"This is Dr Oscar Greyson of the research orbital *Buckland.*" He gripped the edge of the desk to steady himself, to stop the panic from overwhelming him. He tried to remember the required format for emergency broadcasts. It had been years since his company induction. "I am requesting urgent extraction. The station has been compromised. Research assets have been damaged, and lives lost."

The door bucked as something slammed into it, the metal shrieking. Greyson looked from the door to the opening in the ceiling. He had seconds left. Seconds to explain what the security team would be up against.

"Our experiments have resulted in-"

The door tore open with a squeal of metal. Something slammed into Grayson and he screamed as he felt the teeth and claws sink in.

TWO

"What the hell was that?"

Mike Cordero raised a hand for quiet. His team ignored him. They argued amongst themselves in raised voices, gesticulating towards the briefing monitor mounted on the crew compartment wall that showed the final frame of the emergency broadcast.

"It looked like some kind of animal, right?" Black said. He had removed his glasses and was cleaning them on a corner of his shirt, careful not to damage the inbuilt circuitry. He squinted around at the others. "That thing at the end? Had to be some kind of animal."

"Bullshit," Richards drawled. The big man shook his head in disgust. "I ain't never seen any animal move that quick. And I've hunted most kinds. Nah, I reckon someone's been messin' with the broadcast."

"It's a research station, dingus," Black said. "Maybe they've been creating *animals that move that quick.*"

"You think you're being smart, boy?" Richards bristled.

"The footage has to be genuine," Ortega changed the subject. "It will have been run past Lulworth Corp deepfake filters way before being sent to us. If you ask me, I'd say that's a man we just saw attacking the scientist. A big, very fast man, but a man none the less."

Richards sneered. "You think no-one ever figured how to fool deepfake filters before?"

"That's enough," Cordero cut in. He'd let them speculate long enough. It was time to get to the meat of the matter.

Privately, he felt the same way they did. The eight seconds of footage was troubling, even to someone as experienced as Cordero. It raised more questions than it answered, which is why he'd let the team get some of those questions off their chest now, instead of when they were in a potential combat zone.

Questioning Lulworth's capabilities, though, was out of the question. Especially here. Lulworth Rapid Orbital Response shuttles were lousy with hidden cameras. The pilot's cabin, the crew compartment, even the head; everywhere on the *Silverback* would be monitored at all times. It was standard corp policy. The official reasoning was that continuous monitoring ensured working standards were met. The unofficial reason, the true reason, was for HR to weed out potential problem staff before they caused any trouble.

Cordero just wanted to still have a paycheck waiting when they got back to Geneva. ROR team leaders were considered responsible for the 'ethical failings' of their team members.

"We don't know what it is," he continued. "All we know for sure is what Dr Greyson said: the station's compromised, assets are damaged, lives have been lost. This came in four hours ago. Nothing's been heard from the *Buckland* since."

He tapped the monitor. "It doesn't matter if what we just saw was a man, an animal or something else. It doesn't change our mission. We secure the station, figure out what happened, and bring back the black box and any survivors."

"If there are any survivors," Black said. "And assuming we don't get killed by any of those *something else's.*"

"That's why we got these." Richards stroked the Hoeckler-19 squad automatic weapon secured to the compartment wall next to him.

Black shook his head. "Sometimes I worry about you and that gun. You take it to bed with you at night?"

"When your mother ain't available," Richards retorted.

Cordero rolled his eyes. Richards was weird about the SAW, it was true. But he'd met plenty of guys in the service who were just as attached to their weaponry. Compared to them, Richards was pretty normal. Hell, he hadn't even given the gun a name.

Ortega spoke over Black and Richards' bickering, talking directly to Cordero. "Chief, what's the plan?"

"The usual blackout procedure," Cordero said, not bothering to correct the nickname. The rest of the ROR insisted on calling him Chief, despite him never holding a rank like it. "We land at the docks and move as quick as we can to the control deck. We find the mainframe access, pull the black box and head home. Any survivors we find, we bring back with us for debriefing."

"And hostiles?"

"Terminate." Armstrong had been quiet since they'd launched from Geneva. The marksman finally stirred, sitting up from where he'd been lounging in the corner. "With extreme prejudice."

Cordero grinned and nodded at Armstrong. "Couldn't have put it any better myself."

The light above the door to the pilot cabin lit up. A battered speaker mounted on the wall next to it crackled into life.

"Chief, it's MacTiernan. Want to see you up front when you get a minute."

Cordero switched off the briefing monitor. "At ease, gentlemen. Our ETA with the *Buckland* is less than half an hour away. You will have to entertain yourselves until then."

Black was already shuffling a deck of cards. "You want us to deal you in for when you get back?"

Richards snorted. "You know the Chief don't play cards with us mere mortals, Black. He's got actual work to do."

"You think I don't?" Black said. "I've got to tolerate your dumb ass all day. I work harder than your mamma the day after payday at the docks."

Ortega dragged an ammo crate from against the wall to use as a table. "I'm in. Not all us former jarheads are as stuck in the mud as Chief here."

He flashed Cordero a grin. Cordero shook his head, turning away. He had known Ortega for a long time. The man hated gambling. Hated anything that might chip away at his retirement pot. He just played to be sociable. Cordero knew that, when he got back, Ortega would have dropped out of the game without spending more than a couple of dollars.

The cabin door slid open when he approached it, reading the authorization chip in his wrist. He stepped through.

A wall of cigar smoke met him. He coughed, waving a hand in front of his face to clear a path through the smog. The pulsing beats of techno-samba assaulted his eardrums.

"Hey, Chief." MacTiernan yelled from in the pilot's seat, a Cuban clamped between his teeth and an earbud dangling from one ear.

"What's up, Mac?"

MacTiernan jabbed a thumb over his shoulder at the shuttle's windshield. "We're here."

THREE

The *Buckland* was a standard Lulworth modular orbital station, typical of the sort manufactured at the company's plants in low orbit around the globe. It appeared to hang motionless against the vast stillness of space.

The station looked somewhat like a bicycle wheel. A standardized design, the bulbous hub would contain such essential systems as the power and oxygen production facilities, their outputs carried to the slenderer outer rim through a series of spokes that also housed walkways for the crew to access other areas of the station. The rim of the station had been designed to be modular, each section built for a specific task, all joined together into a continuous ring.

Cordero had seen dozens of stations just like the *Buckland* in his time with Lulworth Corp. There was something off about this one, though.

"The power's out?"

MacTiernan sucked on his cigar. The shuttle pilot dialed down the volume on the music thumping from the *Silverback's* cockpit speakers. Cordero felt as though he had been deaf, only to miraculously regain his hearing.

"Looks like it, Chief. We should be seeing a lot more activity around the rim. Radar dishes, cleaning drones, lights through windows. But check it out. Look at the docking module." He pointed with his cigar, spilling ash all over the shuttle dashboard.

Cordero immediately saw the problem.

The *Buckland* was a research station. Lulworth ran a hundred like it, all orbiting just outside the jurisdiction of any legal authorities on Earth. Many were used to test weapons that would otherwise breach international bans. Others were set up to push against the laws around genetic engineering. Their uses were diverse, but all of them - *all* of them - had one thing in common: they were busy places.

"There's nothing happening at the docks," Cordero said.

MacTiernan nodded vigorously. "Right? Look at those docking arms. They're floating loose. The emergency impact sensors - you can see them running along the top of the main hangar door right there - are all off. Something's not right."

"Shouldn't the docking system be running on backup power? These stations all have solar panels to provide power to critical functions even if the main generators go out."

"That's what I'm saying, Chief. Either there's no power *at all* on the station, or someone's cut the docking system off from the grid."

"Why would they do that?"

MacTiernan shrugged. "To stop me from landing?"

"Or to stop anyone else from getting out," Cordero muttered. He leaned back into the crew compartment. "Black, Ortega. Get up here."

"What's up, Chief?" Black said, sauntering past Cordero to stare out of the windshield at the *Buckland.*

"Is that thing completely dark?" Ortega asked.

"Not completely," Black said, before Cordero could reply. The circuitry lining his glasses glowed red as he ran some kind of visual diagnostic. Cordero had never taken the time to understand the tech, but Black swore by his smart glasses. "There are several key systems offline, but there is power. Life support is still on. Oxygen, gravity. The security system's triggered, and holding strong."

"That explains the docking bay doors," MacTiernan said. "If the station is compromised, company security systems will power down the docks. It'll make it tough for us to get onboard though."

"Maybe not," Black mused, turning to the manual console that was mounted on the wall next to a weapons rack. The rack held a single battered shotgun. MacTiernan claimed that he kept it there for emergencies, though Cordero suspected it was for anyone who complained about the music volume.

While Black worked, Ortega had been staring intently at the *Buckland.* "Can you bring us in any closer?" he asked MacTiernan. "Alongside that storage module?"

"Not a problem," MacTiernan said, jostling the throttle. The *Silverback* accelerated violently, instantly reaching speeds that would have killed them all inside Earth's gravity well. They closed on the station; in seconds, the *Buckland* grew to fill the entirety of the view from the cockpit.

"*Dios Mia,*" Ortega said, gripping tightly to the pilot seat headrest. "Did you need to get us here so fast?"

"All part of the service." MacTiernan grinned, exhaling a thick cloud of smoke in Ortega's face.

"What've you seen, Juan?" Cordero stepped in before things got ugly. Ortega was a pretty peaceful guy, for an ex-Recon marine, but he'd never liked the shuttle pilot.

"There. Look." Ortega pointed to a protrusion on the *Buckland's* hull that, from a distance, had been hidden in the shadow of an external water tank.

Cordero frowned. "What the hell is that?"

"Do you remember that search and destroy job we ran in Venezuela, Mike?" Ortega said to Cordero. "We were expecting an illegal oil refinery in the jungle..."

"And instead found the narco-rebels had converted it into a weapons factory," Cordero finished. "Yeah, I remember."

That had been a brutal fight. They'd gone in expecting little more than small arms and the odd rifle. Instead, they'd been faced with rocket launchers and mounted machine guns.

Ortega nodded. "The refinery had been covered in non-standard shit that all looked out of place. Just like that thing. Perhaps the *Buckland's* been modified for some reason."

"But that... modification was hidden," MacTiernan said. "Why hide something in orbit? The reason corps set up these orbitals is so they can do what they like without worrying about national or international law."

There are some things that even corps would want to hide, Cordero thought. He was about to speak when Black exclaimed.

"Got it!" He turned back towards them, a broad smile on his face. "I've got it, guys. Totally got it."

"Got what?" Ortega said, an edge of impatience in his voice.

"A way into the *Buckland*, of course! Mac's right; the security system has shut down power to the docking module." He wagged a finger enthusiastically, as though teaching math to a roomful of bored teenagers. "Luckily for us, though, the docking bay doors are still doors. So, with a little help from the *Silverback's* override protocols, I've convinced the security system that they're a simple doorway that's lost power. The system's protocol will then reroute power through the emergency fallback circuit. You see, all stations like this have-"

"We get it." Cordero raised a hand. If he didn't interrupt, Black would rattle on all day. "You can open the doors."

"Easy as pressing a button." Black tapped the console behind him.

While Black had been talking, MacTiernan had retreated to a more routine distance from the *Buckland.* Now, they hung directly in front of the enormous docking bay doors. Each of its two panels was the size of a football field, made of solid steel ten feet thick. As the team watched, the panels slid apart like a set of monstrous jaws, revealing a yawning darkness beyond.

Cordero patted the grinning Black on the shoulder. "Nice work." He nodded to MacTiernan. "Take us in, Mac."

The pilot stared into the gloom of the docking station, his eyes wide. "On your word, Chief."

FOUR

Ortega took point, as usual. He moved rapidly down the boarding umbilical that connected the *Silverback* to the *Buckland*, his AR-30K held combat ready at his shoulder. The rest of the team followed in wedge formation, Cordero and Armstrong on the flanks and Richards bringing up the rear.

The umbilical ended at an airlock door that led into the docking platform. Ortega stood to one side of it and looked back at Cordero. Cordero nodded.

Ortega slung his rifle over his shoulder and began to turn the manual crank in the wall next to the door. Slowly, the door juddered open.

Cordero couldn't see much of the platform beyond, just vague outlines in the near-dark. A low red glow indicated that the emergency lighting was active, at least.

Ortega slipped through the opening and took cover behind an overturned packing crate. After a moment's glancing around, he raised a hand, palm forwards.

Cordero didn't even need to give the order. The team moved in a fluid, practiced sequence. Richards stepped through the wedge to take up position alongside Ortega, setting up overwatch with his SAW.

Cordero, Armstrong, and Black went next. Cordero on point with Black on his left flank and Armstrong on his right. The marksman moved silently, even his footsteps were muffled. Cordero shivered; the man was a ghost.

He tapped the rig on his belt to send a scrambled radio burst to the *Silverback,* letting MacTiernan know they had safely embarked. Behind him, the airlock cycled closed. MacTiernan would leave the umbilical connected until they returned.

They advanced into the murk. Cordero's breathing sounded loud in his mask. Before connecting to the *Buckland,* Cordero had ordered the team to put on oxygen tanks and ventilators. It was standard operating procedure when boarding a station with a potentially compromised life support system. Just as the apparently useless welding torch strapped to his belt was SOP for hull damage. Richards had complained about the masks, of course. The big man wasn't happy without something to grumble about. But he had grudgingly complied.

Now that he was on board the *Buckland* though, Cordero was starting to think that Richards had a point. The docking platforms on most orbitals were well-lit, to facilitate the transfer of cargo and new arrivals from shuttles to the main body of the station. The *Buckland's* main lights were off, and the platform was shrouded in the lurid red of the emergency lighting. Through the mask's visor, visibility was almost nothing.

The platform looked to have been abandoned in a hurry. Cargo containers had been left half-emptied, some spilling expensive-looking laboratory equipment across the bare steel floor.

Halfway across the platform, Cordero heard Armstrong hiss over the squad communicator. It was their team code; a single short hiss to get the others' attention. Cordero enforced a no communication rule in combat zones.

Cordero slowed, letting Black move into the point position. Once the specialist had advanced a few yards, Cordero shrugged at Armstrong. *What's up?*

The sniper was kneeling, DMR combat ready. He nodded to something at his feet. Cordero moved in for a closer look.

There was a broad, shallow pockmark in the steel floor. There were two more a few inches away.

Armstrong looked a question at Cordero, who nodded.

They were impact marks. From bullets.

Cordero raised his right hand, fingers splayed out, then rotated his wrist ninety degrees. He heard a series of rapid tongue clicks on the comm in response. The team understood; this was a hot zone, stay alert.

Things were starting to look interesting.

Black, against protocol, had continued his advance and had reached an open cargo door on the far side of the docking platform. Biting back a reprimand, Cordero led Armstrong to take up position alongside Black.

He glanced cautiously around the door frame, being careful to minimize his profile. As per the standard Lulworth orbital design, the docking module - like all the external modules - was connected to the station rim, which contained nothing but a broad arterial corridor that linked each modular section. Like the docking platform, the corridor was shrouded in darkness.

Ortega and Richards moved up to join them as Armstrong and Black took up covering positions around the doorway. Ortega stopped to stare at a dark patch on the wall. He gestured Cordero over.

"What is it?" Cordero asked, a final glance satisfying him that their position was secure for the moment.

Ortega activated the flashlight mounted on his shoulder and directed the beam towards the dark patch. It was a dark, glossy red.

"Blood," Ortega said softly.

"Something else over here too, Chief," Black said, from where he knelt by the door frame. He pointed at three long, thin marks in the steel, that ran along the wall at chest height.

"More bullet impacts?" Ortega said, directing the light at the markings.

"No. Too narrow." Cordero leaned in closer. There was another smear of blood in one of the grooves "These look almost like..."

"Claw marks," Richards said from behind him, resting the SAW easily on his hip.

"Right."

"Sure," Ortega scoffed. "What kinda thing has claws that can tear steel?"

"Nothin' I ever want to meet." Richards spat a globule of phlegm onto the floor.

Cordero stood. He looked at his team. They remained alert, careful; weapons held ready. But he could see wide eyes through their visors. Richards's words had spooked them.

"Whatever it is," he said, "we can deal with it." He racked the slide on his 37K. "We've got the guns, we've got the skills. Whatever's come to this station, they'll soon be wishing they hadn't."

"Hoo-rah," Ortega said. Richards and Black just laughed.

"Black," Cordero snapped. The tech straightened. "Which way to the control deck?"

"Uh..." Black's eyes became unfocused as he scanned through the reams of data being beamed directly into his retinas from his glasses. "We need to move counter to the station's spin. So, that way." He gestured down the arterial corridor.

"On me, keep it loose." Cordero set off without waiting for the others, knowing they would follow.

He advanced confidently into the gloom, determined to show the team not a hint of fear. When he had been a soldier - a proper soldier, a recon marine - nothing had scared him more than following someone with no idea about what they were doing. When he'd been given a squad of his own, his commanding officer had taught him the secret of effective leadership: always act like you know exactly what is going on, even if you don't have a clue.

There was a shape on the floor ahead of them. It looked like a pile of rags that had been left in the center of the corridor. As Cordero got closer, he saw that it was a body.

It had been a man, he thought, though it was hard to tell with so much of their face and torso missing. They wore the ragged remains of a white lab coat, now soaked red. One arm had been torn off at the elbow and lay several feet away.

"Woah," Black said. He stopped next to Cordero, swallowing hard. "Who would do that to a person?"

Ortega knelt beside the corpse, stepping into the pool of blood surrounding it. Juan had always had a stomach of iron, Cordero remembered, even before getting into Recon and seeing some of the shit they'd seen. "Chief, you remember that time in Colombia, when we chased those guys into the jungle?"

Cordero smiled. "You mean when you ran your dumb ass straight into an ambush and got shot in the leg, and I had to carry you back to the chopper, with you whining the whole way?"

Ortega grinned. "I still owe you for that. No, this was before that. We were following a set of tracks, hoping they'd lead us to the rebel's base. Instead, we caught up with the guy who'd been leaving them."

"Or what was left of him." Cordero grimaced at the memory. "He'd wound up killed by a jaguar."

"Right, right." Ortega nodded at the corpse. "Killed and eaten. Just like this guy."

FIVE

The team reached the *Buckland's* control deck without finding any more bodies. They did find more evidence of violence during their march: part of the arterial corridor was blocked by a hastily assembled barricade of overturned filing cabinets and tables from a nearby canteen. One of the cabinets was riddled with bullet holes and there were scorch marks on a wall that looked like the aftermath of a small detonation. Cordero hoped that whoever had caused an explosion on an orbital station was already dead; he didn't want to run across anyone that crazy.

The team were unsettled by Ortega's observation about the dead body. The quiet of the station was getting to them too. Cordero had been on dozens of Lulworth orbitals. They weren't large, and the company had no concern for safe occupancy levels. The background noise common to all stations was the day-to-day lives of people, crammed together.

The *Buckland* was dead silent.

Black had kept up an endless chatter since the body, commenting on every single thing that they saw, no matter how commonplace. Richards grumbled at the patter, though Cordero suspected he was relieved to have the distraction.

Cordero allowed them to bicker, despite his no talking rule. He wanted them to take their minds off what they'd seen. He had relented on requiring them to wear masks, too. Whatever had happened on the *Buckland,* it wasn't an airborne virus.

You're not in Recon now, he reminded himself. Former mercenaries like Richards and Black are going to get freaked out by little things, like finding a half-eaten body.

The control deck was locked down. It took Black five long minutes to manually override the entrance doors.

"Our override codes aren't working," he complained. "Either someone has been messing with the security system to keep us out, or the station's clearance is way above ours."

With the door finally open, Ortega led Richards and Armstrong in to secure the room. After a moment, he gave the all clear.

Cordero followed Black to an untidy desk, cluttered with paperwork and candy bar wrappers. The technician swept the mess aside and plugged a handheld unit into the console.

"This is odd," he said, after a moment of tapping on the unit's keyboard.

"What's up?" Cordero had been scanning the room for clues. Aside from an almost deliberate disregard for the corporate clear desk policy, the control deck looked like all the others he'd seen. It was circular, with desks lining the walls. The center of the room was dominated by the station's massive mainframe servers, through which all the *Buckland's* data flowed. It included the black box hard drives which securely backed up all the station's system activity.

"Our override codes aren't working here either." Black turned the portable unit so that Cordero could see the display. The screen showed a garbled combination of numbers, letters and symbols that meant nothing to Cordero.

"You can't access anything at all?"

Black tapped a key firmly and the portable unit's screen cleared. At the same time, the control console came to life, displaying what looked to Cordero like the standard Lulworth operating system.

"Oh no, I can access *some* systems," Black continued, gesturing to a series of icons on the console. "Basic stuff like life support, security, maintenance bots, that sort of thing. I can even get the docks back up and running from here. But the whole reason ROR teams have overrides is to let them pull the black box. And *that's* what's locked down, tighter than a nun on the Fourth of July."

"Can you access it any other way?"

"I can try." Black sucked his teeth. "It will take time though. And I can't make any guarantees. I've never seen this kind of encryption before."

"Why would the company create a black box so secure that its own retrieval team couldn't get to it?" Ortega said from across the room.

"Goddamn corporate assholes," Richards spat. "So worried about losing their market advantage, they throw away the key to their own data."

"This encryption is a real bitch," Black said, typing rapidly. "It's just going to take a few hours to crack."

"A few hours?" Cordero shook his head. "Is there a faster way?"

Black stopped typing. He leaned back in the chair and looked up at Cordero. "Not from here, but someone at this station has to have clearance. If we can find one of them and bring them here, then all our problems are over." He clicked his fingers. "Like that."

"So, we're talking about a senior executive," Cordero said. "Are there any on this station?"

Black consulted the console again. "We're in luck, Chief. There's a corporate visit scheduled for today. A senior exec named, ah, Elaine Markovitz, should be on the station now."

"Looks like the visit's cancelled." Cordero unslung his rifle from his shoulder. "Where is she now?"

"The locator in her wrist implant is showing her in the labs complex. Lab B7."

"Is she alive?"

Black sucked his teeth. "Hard to tell. She's not moving, but these corporate types don't get much cardio. She's with a bunch of other staff. None of them are moving, either."

That sounded bad to Cordero. "Will her wrist implant give us access to the black box?"

"Provided she's important enough, sure."

"Alright." Cordero patted Black on the shoulder then turned to the others. "We're moving out."

"Lab B7?" Ortega said from across the room.

"Lab B7. We're bringing back Ms. Markovitz. Black, I want you to stay here, keep working on breaking into the black box. See if you can get us access to the lab complex too."

"No problem, Chief. I can open a path from here."

"You're leaving him here on his own?" Richards said. "Little man can barely look out for himself. What if something tries to eat him, too?"

Black patted his AR-37K, propped against the desk. "I can take care of myself, Richards."

"Not with that little girl's gun, you can't."

"He will be fine, Richards," Cordero cut in. "Come on, we need to move if we ever want to get off this orbital."

"Where is the comms room the emergency message was sent from?" Armstrong asked in his chilly monotone.

"Um." Black tapped away. "It's adjoining the labs complex."

"Near any lab in particular?"

"Yes," Black said, a frown creasing his brow at what he saw on the screen. "Lab B7."

SIX

Nothing about this mission felt right to Cordero. As he followed Ortega through the *Buckland* arterial, he was struck again at how empty the station felt.

He had been on the orbital *Deloitte* when the station had experienced a critical reactor failure. Cordero's team had been one of a dozen dispatched by the company to evacuate the station and, more critically, secure samples of the valuable gene-spliced corn being developed on board.

When they arrived, they found a riot in process. Half of the *Deloitte's* crew blamed the other half for the disaster. A few crossed words and a fistfight or two had led to a full-scale war breaking out. Cordero had stepped onto a docking platform covered in blood. They had found dozens of dead on the route to the agricultural growth centers. Everywhere they looked, there were dead men and women. A few children too, who had been born on board. Crew babies, they called them.

The *Buckland* was different. Here, the crew had vanished almost completely. Aside from the evidence of shooting they'd found, and the partially eaten corpse, there was no sign of anyone.

Cordero had thought the *Deloitte* was the worst mission he'd been on. Already, the *Buckland* felt far worse.

The locked black box was the latest mystery to add to his sense of unease. It was standard for such files to be encrypted - the company didn't make a habit of trusting anyone, not even their own retrieval teams - but for them to be locked out of accessing the box itself made no sense.

Cordero had never found himself in this kind of situation before, and he didn't like it.

"Something's off about this whole job, man," Richards said, echoing Cordero's thoughts. "They send us to bring back a box then lock it away? I don't like this at all."

"You don't have to like it, Richards," Ortega said from his position a dozen meters ahead. Now that they'd removed their face masks, they could speak without their squad communication equipment. Ortega's voice echoed strangely off the bare steel walls. "You just need to follow orders. Let the Chief do the thinking."

Cordero wasn't comfortable with Ortega laying down the law on his behalf, but he didn't contradict it. The team put their faith in him because he made good decisions that kept them alive, not just because he was one step above them in the corporate pay structure.

Instead, he decided to be frank with them, let them know his thinking. "I agree with you, Richards. Something is up."

Richards grunted, surprised that Cordero agreed with him. "So, what're we gonna do about it?"

"Finding Markovitz should give us some answers."

"Markovitz, hell." Richards barked a laugh. "I vote we ditch this job, head back to the shuttle and leave this place alone."

"You scared, big guy?" Armstrong's voice was little more than a whisper from the shadows. "That ain't like you."

"Course I ain't scared." Richards turned to glare at the marksman. "We've both been in worse places than this. Remember Jakarta?"

Armstrong nodded, but said no more. Cordero wondered what the story was there. Richards and

Armstrong had worked mercenary jobs before joining the ROR at Lulworth, but they didn't talk much about it.

Everyone has their own past, he supposed. He and Ortega were no different.

"But what I'm sayin'," Richards continued, "is that we work to a system, right? We got processes and procedures for every job we take on. And what we're doin' now, looking for this Markovitz, is standard procedure, right? It's SOP."

"Is there a point to all this?" Ortega asked. He had stopped, turning to face Richards. Cordero barked at him to keep his eyes forward, making a mental note to start running some of his old drills with the team again, once they got back to Earth. Ortega was getting sloppy. He'd never have pulled a move like that in Recon.

Richards smirked. "The point is, none of this is standard, right? SOP don't apply."

"SOP always applies," Cordero said. "I'm not bailing because things here are a little spooky-"

"Spooky? Hell, that guy had his face bitten off-"

"Things here are *a little spooky*," Cordero said firmly. "But we can deal with it. We're not leaving till we've done whatever we can. But I'm not risking our jobs just because things are getting... strange."

"You're fine with risking us then," Richards grumbled.

"No, I'm not. That's why we're sticking to standard procedures. They reduce risk. That's the point."

"Sometimes you gotta make your own decisions, Chief."

"I *am* making my own decision here, Richards. This is my decision. We're going to find the exec. If you don't like it, head on back to the *Silverback*. Alone. Then, when we get back to Geneva, I'll put that in my report."

That shut Richards up. The threat of a poor quarterly performance report put the fear of God into any

Lulworth employee, from ROR teams to the CEO. Richards loved to complain, but he loved getting paid his performance bonus even more.

They walked on in silence for a while. The arterial was featureless and empty. They didn't find any more signs of violence, which unnerved Cordero more than a room full of corpses.

They had just passed a sign labelled 'Water Storage' when the temperature dropped. Cordero suddenly found himself shivering. He felt as though he had walked through an icy waterfall.

Cordero activated his radio. "Black, what the hell's going on?"

"Not my fault, Chief." Black's voice came back tinny and distorted through the earbud. "Looks like a few systems are on the fritz. You're lucky you're not in the crew cabins; they're overheating. I'm trying to switch on the sprinklers to cool things down."

"Hey, Chief," Ortega said, overhearing on the squad comms. "Sounds a little like those weeks we spent in the Arizona desert, remember? Hot all day and freezing at night."

"What were you doing in the desert?" Black asked.

"Working on a rodeo. Long story." Cordero grimaced. "Anyway, how are the labs looking?"

"All good." Black sounded excited. "The whole lab complex had been locked down."

"Shit," Armstrong hissed. "Bad news."

"Nah. Looked like a rush job by someone desperate, not something the system did by itself."

"It's open now?"

"Sure is." Cordero could hear Black grinning through the comms. "I couldn't just open up B7, though. I had to crack open the whole complex instead."

"So long as we can get access. Good work, Black." Cordero shut down the link.

"Speak of the devil," Ortega called. "Lab's coming up."

Cordero raised his hand for quiet. Up ahead, on the left, were a pair of scarred bulkhead doors. They were partially open. In the bottom corner of one, Cordero saw a smear of blood, shockingly red against the gunmetal grey of the bulkhead.

Cordero, Richards, and Armstrong stacked to the left of the door. Ortega stood by the lock pad on the opposite side. It flashed green, unlocked. Just as Black had promised.

Cordero nodded.

They moved through the door in good, practiced order, rifles raised as they scanned the corners. They entered a short dark hallway. A set of steel stairs descended on the far end, harsh white lighting leaching up from below.

Cordero took the lead. He heard the rest of the team following behind him. He stopped at the top of the stairs. Ortega appeared at his side. Cordero nodded to his friend; together, they moved cautiously forward.

Cordero descended the stairs, taking one step at a time. He moved carefully, making as little sound as possible. Ortega followed closely behind.

As Cordero got closer to the bottom, a larger room came into view. The white lighting got even harsher, blasting out from a pair of strip lights hanging from a tall ceiling. Twin lines of whitewashed columns marched down the center of the room and a steel frame balcony cast a shadow over the entryway.

As Cordero crossed the threshold a few meters behind Ortega, a sense of wrongness washed over him. He opened his mouth to speak, when something ricocheted off the wall, inches from his head. He ducked instinctively.

The sound of a gunshot broke the silence.

SEVEN

Cordero was moving before he could register what was happening. He shouted a warning then took cover against the entryway wall.

More shots sounded. From the balcony, he realized. Luckily, the angle was bad, though that would also make it hard to return fire.

He leaned out anyway, fanning the AR-30K's trigger, hosing the balcony with bullets. He wasn't trying to hit anything, just making sure the shooter kept their head down.

"Moving up!" Ortega rushed past him, head down, taking advantage of Cordero's suppressive fire to seek a better angle. He pressed himself against the closest whitewashed pillar and nodded to Cordero, breathing fast.

A figure stepped out from behind another pillar, clad in black fatigues and body armor, face hidden behind a mask and visor. Corporate commandos, Cordero guessed.

The assault rifle in the commando's hands was aimed at Ortega. Cordero opened his mouth to warn Ortega. The booming return of a gunshot cut him off.

The commando staggered backwards, clutching at their neck. A second shot shattered their visor and sent them to the floor in a spray of blood.

Cordero, ears ringing, turned to see Armstrong sighting down his DMR, the barrel hot. "Nice work," he muttered. The marksman simply nodded in response.

"Ortega, look out!" Richards bellowed.

Two more commandos appeared from behind the other columns. One, a muscular giant to rival Richards, was screaming obscenities in heavily accented English as he fired a salvo of shots from the hip, forcing Ortega to hunker down. The other racked an automatic shotgun added to the fire pouring onto Ortega.

"Richards, get up there and help him. Armstrong, covering fire."

Not waiting for a response, Cordero stepped out and fired up at the balcony. Simultaneously, Armstrong switched his DMR to auto and emptied the magazine in a wide arc towards the new attackers, driving them into cover.

Richards moved quickly for a man of his size, even encumbered with the SAW. He ran up alongside Ortega and, without pausing to catch a breath, readied the SAW at his hip, turned towards the ambushers, and pressed the trigger.

The room was filled with the roar of the SAW as it rattled off high caliber bullets, tearing chunks out of the columns. Richards had a broad grin on his face as he fired. Cordero shook his head. That man sure loved his work.

Something heavy bounced off the wall near the entryway. "Grenade!" Armstrong yelled.

Cordero was already moving. He took three sprinter's steps, then flung himself up the stairs with all the strength he could muster.

A wave of force picked him up and slammed him chest-first into the steel stairs. A percussive *boom* wiped away all sound. Fragments of shrapnel tore into the back of his calves.

Cordero rolled onto his back, wincing. Armstrong stood over him, looking unfazed. The marksman extended a hand.

"Let's go, Chief."

Standing, Cordero picked up his rifle and ran back down the stairs. Ortega and Richards were still exchanging fire with the two commandos. The gunfight had reached a stalemate, neither side able to maneuver to get a better position on the other.

For the first time, Cordero noted a closed door in the wall behind Ortega. A problem for later, he thought. Right now, we have to deal with this grenade-throwing maniac.

Almost on cue, a figure leaned over the edge of the balcony, another grenade clutched in their hand. Cordero was ready this time. He squeezed the trigger.

Armstrong was quicker. The DMR boomed again, hitting the grenadier right between the eyes. They fell backwards, out of sight.

Cordero heard the grenade bounce on the floor above them, followed by a muffled curse.

The blast knocked him to his knees. A wave of heat washed over his face. The underside of the balcony tore open, the metal unfurling like the petals of an inverted flower.

Two down, two to go, thought Cordero.

The muscular commando seemed taken aback by the blast. When the grenade went off, he had been leaning out to fire at Richards. Now he stared, slack-jawed, at the ruins of the balcony.

Richards didn't waste the opportunity. Forgetting the SAW, he lunged out from cover to rush the dazed attacker. He was so focused on his target that he forgot about the shotgun-wielding commando. As he moved out of cover, the shotgunner emerged, firing.

The first shots missed. Richards didn't even notice as clouds of shot whistling around him.

As the commando was lining up to fire again, Ortega cut their legs out from under them with a burst of automatic fire. The commando toppled forwards, screaming, twisting towards Ortega as they fell.

Ortega advanced, lining up a kill shot.

The door behind him opened. Ortega, intent on the wounded shotgunner, didn't notice as another commando emerged. They were unarmed and moved with a limp, but were closing fast on Ortega's blind side.

A cold rage filled Cordero. Adrenaline spiked through his system. Before he realized what he was doing, he had reached the injured commando in a few fast steps. The man glanced around, eyes widening when he saw Cordero approaching.

Cordero dove forwards and tackled the man to the ground. He heard a grunt of pain as they landed, noticing that there were bloody bandages around the man's chest. He pulled back a fist, blood singing, and swung.

The injured man bucked beneath him, jolting Cordero over onto his right side. Quick as a snake, the commando rolled smoothly into a standing position, pulling a knife from his boot.

"Fuck you, pal," the man hissed through gritted teeth. He came at Cordero, swinging the blade. Cordero stepped back, dodging the first swing, then the second.

The third grazed his bicep. The commando bubbled a laugh and swung again.

Cordero blocked the blow with his forearm. The force of the impact sent the knife spinning out of the man's grip.

The man glanced after the blade. Taking advantage of his distraction, Cordero stepped in and brought his forehead down onto the man's mask.

Pain blossomed across Cordero's face. His vision blurred. But he was rewarded with the crunch of bone. The commando screamed, stumbling backwards, one hand slapping blindly at his waist where he had a pistol holstered.

He dove for the knife, his fingers closing around it at the same time the commando got the pistol free. With no time to properly draw a bead, Cordero threw the blade.

The pistol clattered to the floor. The commando fell to his knees, the knife protruding from his throat.

Cordero walked over to the dying man. "Fuck *you*, pal." He pulled the knife free. The commando collapsed bonelessly to the floor, choking on his own blood.

Cordero noticed the room had gone silent, except for a sound like a man punching a wet speed bag. Cordero looked up.

The commando with the shotgun was dead, a hole in their visor, a widening pool of blood around them. The ruins of the balcony still smoked, flames licking at the shattered framework.

Richards knelt on the chest of the big commando and was methodically slamming his huge fists into the man's red ruin of a face. The man's hands were drumming weakly on Richards's legs. As Cordero watched, Richards grasped the man's head and smashed it into the floor; once, twice, then a third and final time. The man went limp. Richards climbed off him, wiping bloody hands on his fatigues.

Cordero knelt to look at the body of one of the dead commandos. Like the others, the man's outfit was stripped of any identifying markings, not even a corporate logo. His rifle was a mass-produced AR with the serial numbers filed off.

Cordero called Ortega over. "Notice anything about these guys?"

Ortega shrugged. "From the gear and the getup, I'd say they're from one of Lulworth's rivals. I'd guess they're to blame for the hatchet job on the security system."

Cordero grunted in agreement. He pointed to the man he'd killed. "Did you see that some are wounded?"

Ortega did a double take. "Damn, you're right. I hadn't noticed. Those bandages look recent."

"This one has them too." Armstrong's monotone whisper came from over by the dead shotgunner. The man had a bandage wound around his shoulder, and another on his bicep, which Armstrong was in the process of unwrapping.

He peered at the wound. "Looks like a bite mark."

"A what?" Richards joined them. Specks of blood covered his face like freckles. He looked over Armstrong's shoulder. "Goddam, you're right. Some animal's taken a chunk out of his arm. A big animal, too."

"Do they have animal cargo on this station?" Ortega asked.

Cordero shook his head. "I think we can assume that whatever did this also ate the civilian we found earlier. Whatever happened here, I don't think it was just down to these commandos. I say we-"

He was interrupted by a low moan from beneath the rubble of the balcony. The team looked at one another.

"Move that shit."

Richards and Armstrong hauled the wreckage aside. Cordero dug underneath; his searching hands found fabric, damp and sticky. Then, he found what felt like flesh.

There was another moan.

"Get a light over here," he ordered. Ortega hurried to comply, shining the beam beneath the rubble.

Cordero could make out the figure of a man. He was dressed in the same black, featureless fatigues as the others, darker in patches where blood was soaking into the material. He wore no mask. The torchlight shone on his face; he was an older man, Cordero guessed he was in his fifties. His hair was white where it wasn't stained with blood and buzzed short. An ugly scar ran down from his brow to the corner of his lip. His eyelids twitched as the light passed over them and he gave another pained moan.

"We've got a live one," Cordero said. "Get this thing off him."

With a concerted effort, the four of them managed to haul the mass of twisted metal aside.

Ortega dropped to the man's side and opened a med pack. He took the man's pulse with one hand while searching through the pack's contents with the other.

"Pulse is weak. He's alive, but he's hurt. And out cold."

Richards spat. "So we leave him. If we're going to find Markovitz, we should get on with it."

"Damn straight," Armstrong agreed. "I can put a bullet in him now."

"We take him with us," Cordero said.

"Come *on,* Chief!" Richards exclaimed. "You said yourself, we stick to SOP. Babysitting some wounded asshole ain't standard procedure."

"He can tell us what happened here."

"So can Markovitz!" Richards threw his arms up in the air. "I thought that's what we were here for, to find some exec so they can tell us what happened."

"Whatever happened," Cordero said firmly, staring unwaveringly at Richards, "this man's team were at least partially responsible for it. Markovitz can probably only tell us half the story. For the rest, we need to get it from this guy."

Richards, his face red with rage, opened his mouth to reply.

A bloodcurdling roar echoed through the room.

EIGHT

"What the hell was that?"

Everyone began talking at once. Even Armstrong, usually so taciturn, began to curse under his breath. Cordero shouted for quiet, but nobody was paying him any attention.

The roar came again. Louder this time. Closer. Cordero felt his guts clench with fear at the sound. It was animal, and ancient in a way he couldn't fully understand. For a moment, he wasn't a veteran Marine, he was a prey creature cowering in its den.

"It's coming from the arterial, back the way we came," Ortega said. The expression on his face made him look like he'd seen a ghost. His rifle hung loosely at his side.

"What the hell was that?" Richards repeated. He looked around at the others, his eyes wide and white. His brow was beaded with sweat, despite the cold.

"I... I don't know." Cordero wished he had a better answer. His muscles felt locked in position. He took a swallow of air, counted to four, held for four, then exhaled slowly.

"We need to get out of here, man." Panic tinged Ortega's voice. He began backing away from the stairs.

"Wait," Cordero croaked. His heart rate had returned to something resembling normal. The fear had passed, for now at least. He knew what he had to do next: force the others to fall back on their training. "We're leaving. Together. On me," he said, in his best drill instructor tone.

It seemed to have the desired effect. Ortega stood straighter, his eyes focusing. Even the two ex-mercenaries fell into something resembling order.

"Armstrong, on point. Lead us to the labs," he snapped. "Richards, bring the wounded."

Richards frowned. "None of us are wounded, Chief."

"The commando." Cordero pointed to where the injured man lay amongst the wreckage of the balcony. "You're the only one who can carry him. Ortega, watch his back."

But Richards didn't move. He grimaced, showing broad white teeth. "You've gotta be kidding me!"

Cordero suppressed a sigh. He should have anticipated this. "You know I'm not joking, Richards. Pick him up."

"That son of a bitch tried to kill us, man!"

"I don't care." Cordero didn't move and didn't look away. That unnerved Richards; a man his size got used to people being intimidated by him. He didn't know how to react when others stood their ground. "Pick him up."

"I don't believe this," Richards spat. "You're gonna slow us down to save this piece of shit?" He slammed a fist against his chest. "I say we leave him here to die."

"We don't leave anyone to die. Now do your job and pick him up."

Richards turned suddenly and stormed towards Cordero. He didn't stop until his face was inches from Cordero's. His eyes were wide and crazed; bursting blood vessels bunched in their corners.

Cordero didn't flinch. He stared back at Richards, unblinking, a faint smile on his face.

He realized that the smile wasn't faked. His heart was hammering, his muscles were taught for action, and excitement surged through his blood.

What was wrong with him? He was facing down one of his own men, in a situation that was completely breaking down, and he was *excited?*

Is this what I am? he thought. An adrenaline junkie looking for the next fix. The next fight.

He was supposed to be a soldier. A leader. What should a leader do in this situation?

"Fine, I'll carry him," he said. He put a hand on Richards's chest and pushed him firmly away. Richards stepped aside, looking surprised.

Cordero blinked, suddenly tired. Slinging the AR over his shoulder, he nodded towards the bulkhead. "Armstrong, you go ahead. I'll catch up." He knelt alongside the unconscious man.

The roar came again. Closer this time. It sounded like it was right outside the lab doors.

Cordero looked around at the others. "Move it, *now!"*

He tucked his hands under the man's shoulders and hauled him backwards, dragging him from the pile of rubble. Blood still covered the man's face and clothing but, thankfully, none of it was the bright red of arterial blood.

There was a noticeable absence of noise behind him. He looked back over his shoulder.

Richards still stood there, watching him.

"You better have a good reason for not following my orders," he growled.

The big man stepped forwards. "I think we should make a stand here. We can use these pillars for cover. And that wrecked balcony will slow down whatever's coming."

Cordero stood, dusting his hands on his pants legs. "You think we should stand and fight?"

"For sure," Richards nodded. "It's what we do."

"What we do, Richards, is our jobs." He gestured towards the stairs. "We have no idea what is coming. For all we know, the pillars, the wreckage - hell, even our weapons - might not stop it. We don't know what we're up against. But finding out isn't our job. What is our job, Richards?"

Richards looked away. "Recovering the black box."

"Damn straight. Now, if you're not going to help me, go join the others."

Instead, Richards lifted the unconscious man as easily as though he were a newborn baby. He slung the burden over one shoulder with no pretense of being gentle, then carried the commando with him to the bulkhead where Ortega and Armstrong waited.

Ortega opened the door. A corridor led away, lit by the same harsh white lighting as the room they were currently in.

Wordlessly, Armstrong took the lead. Richards followed behind at a safe distance, avoiding meeting Cordero's eyes.

Ortega slapped the lock pad on the door then fell in beside Cordero. "The big lug finally saw sense, then?"

"Of a kind. Took a little persuasion on my part."

"You're good at that." Ortega laughed. "I remember that girl in Buenos Ares-"

"Not this again," Cordero groaned. But he smiled when he said it. He remembered the girl Ortega was talking about. Maria, she had been called. She'd worked in a bar near the base. Every marine had listed after her, but she refused all offers. Until Cordero had come along. "That was nothing to do with persuasion. That was my natural sex appeal."

"That wouldn't work on Richards?"

Cordero snorted. "God, I hope not."

"Would you go back to Recon?" Ortega asked, suddenly serious.

"What, and leave all this behind?" Cordero spread his arms wide to gesture at the bare corridor.

"Nah, me neither." Ortega looked away wistfully. "You see, I got a plan."

"I know all about your plan, Juan," Cordero said. "How far off are you from buying that farm?"

Ortega sucked his teeth, thinking. "I've got two more years of this shit. Two more years before I can afford to retire. Then, I'm out. I'm gonna find myself a good woman to care for me while I look after the cows and grow corn. Hell, maybe I'll have a kid or two, and never look at another gun again."

"Here's to the good life," Cordero said. He unhooked his canteen. Ortega did the same. They clinked them together, then each took a long swig of water.

Ortega smacked his lips. "Retired at thirty-five. That's the way to do it."

"Careful, man," Cordero said. "You're tempting fate with talk like that."

Ortega laughed. "You really know how to ruin the mood, you know?"

"Funny, that's what the girl in Buenos Ares told me too."

NINE

Cordero kept the team moving at a brisk pace, following the signs towards lab B7. The roaring behind them continued, though the acoustics of the station made it hard to tell if it was getting closer or further away. The sound certainly pushed the team to move faster.

Armstrong ranged ahead, sometimes disappearing around a corner, but always returning to keep the others in view. Ortega had left Cordero's side to cover the marksman, keeping a watchful eye on Richards.

Richards kept up a string of profanity as he marched, most of it directed at the unconscious commando that he carried. Twice, he stopped and seemed to consider dumping his burden to the floor, before thinking better of it and continuing.

Cordero made a mental note to check Richards's records once they were back in the Geneva office, to see if there were any instances of subordination from before Cordero joined the team. The smart thing to do would have been to check before now, but he had joined the team from outside the company, at Ortega's recommendation. Ortega had vouched for Richards, and Cordero had ignored his usual caution in favor of trusting his old friend's opinion. Next time he joined a new team he would check everyone's records, he promised himself. Caution had always been his watchword; it hadn't steered him wrong before.

Richards had always been belligerent, but that had been an asset to Cordero, until now. He had known that the man had ambitions to lead a ROR team of his own. Lulworth liked to encourage competition in its staff.

Management was indifferent to the methods their employees used to obtain promotions, so Cordero had always kept a careful watch on Richards. But, until now, he had never reacted so aggressively.

It must be the stress of the situation, Cordero decided, as they rounded a corner onto another bland corridor. Here, they finally had a break from the clinical lighting; the lights were broken, smashed. Cordero could make out a junction up ahead.

For all of Richards's bluster on the subject, the former mercenary was far more comfortable when following established company procedures than using his initiative. The strange circumstances of the mission - the missing crew, the commando team, and especially the terrifying roaring - had meant that suddenly SOP seemed less standard than it had before.

Cordero had learned through harsh, brutal experience that rules didn't always look the same when they came into contact with the enemy. Recon had taught him that. Richards, despite all his years guarding oil refineries across the southern states of the US and Southeast Asia, had never learnt that lesson.

"Looks like B7 is up ahead." Armstrong's voice buzzed in his earpiece.

"Good. Go ahead and secure the entrance."

The marksman nodded and entered the darkness around the junction.

Cordero quickened his pace until he was beside Richards. Seeing this, Ortega dropped back to join them, forming a guard on either side. They followed Armstrong into the gloom.

Glass crunched beneath Cordero's boots. Strange, he thought, that the lights would have blown here, but not elsewhere in the labs.

He could see Armstrong's outline ahead, flanked on either side by the deeper pits of darkness where other corridors joined the junction.

Flanked on either side...

Oh no. "Ambush!" he roared.

Something large darted at Armstrong from one side. It moved fast, impossibly fast. Armstrong turned, his rifle already raised. The thing crashed into him, sending him to the floor.

Something gleamed in the dark. *Were those...claws?*

Armstrong screamed.

TEN

Everything happened at once.

Ortega started firing, the sound of his assault rifle shockingly loud in the enclosed space. By his muzzle flare, Cordero could see what had attacked Armstrong.

It looked like a lizard. But he had never seen a lizard that big before. It was bigger than even the Komodo dragons he'd seen at a zoo during his last shore leave. Its stiff tail whipped back and forth as it tore into Armstrong's abdomen with its wickedly curved talons, pulling loose coils of intestine.

Armstrong was screaming, high and loud. Blood spewed from his mouth and ran down his chin. He batted at the creature's long snout, trying to dislodge its head from within his guts. As Cordero watched, the lizard snapped its head up and bit one of Armstrong's hands clean off at the wrist.

Cordero realized that he was shooting. His index finger was curled tightly around the trigger of his AR. The rifle bucked in his hands, not designed for sustained firing.

Richards was firing too, the unconscious commando lay discarded at his feet. The percussive roar of his SAW thundered over the rattle of the ARs.

A bullet smacked into the lizard's forelimb with a wet *thunk*. The creature was sent sprawling, shrieking to the floor.

Richards moved towards Armstrong, bellowing wordless cries of anger. But the monster was already back on its feet. It hissed at Richards, revealing rows of needle-sharp teeth. It crouched, readying to pounce.

Cordero turned his rifle towards it when the magazine ran dry. He cursed; he'd emptied it without realizing. Such a rookie error.

Fumbling at his belt for a replacement magazine, Cordero saw movement out of the corner of his eyes. Fast moving shapes closed on them from either side.

Ortega saw them too. He switched on his shoulder-mounted flashlight, blinding Cordero for a brief second. When his vision cleared, he could see more of the monsters surrounding them. Hisses and roars warned him that more were coming.

"We have to get out of here!"

Then, his eardrums were hammered by the sound of the SAW being fired on fully automatic.

Richards stood over Armstrong's twitching body, his legs wide in a bracing position. The SAW bucked in his grip as it poured out a torrent of fully automatic fire.

One of the giant lizards was torn apart by the barrage, exploding in a welter of gore. But even as it died, another leapt from the shadows, hind claws raised to disembowel Richards.

Cordero yelled, but the big man was already turning. He swung the SAW like a bat, clubbing the creature in mid-leap. Something cracked wetly, and the lizard crashed into the nearby wall, where it slid to the ground and lay still.

Another lizard closed on Richards from behind. Overbalanced with the swing, Richards dropped the SAW to stop himself falling, instead raising his fists and turning towards the approaching threat.

Cordero sensed movement behind him. He swung his empty rifle in a tight arc. A sudden impact jolted his arms, and he was rewarded with a screech of pain.

Turning, he was faced with two lizards. The first clawed at its bloody muzzle. That must have been the one he'd hit. The other hissed, scratching at him with its talons.

It moved blindingly fast. Cordero just managed to raise his rifle across his chest before the beast struck. The force knocked Cordero backwards and the rifle was ripped from his grasp. The creature turned to watch it fall, tilting its head to one side like a curious bird.

Before it returned its attention to him, Cordero whipped his hunting knife from his belt and lunged forwards. The cold steel slid easily through the flesh on the creature's neck, causing it to leap backwards, trailing ribbons of hot blood.

It landed awkwardly, tried to stagger forwards, then fell on its side. Blood pulsed thickly from the wound in its neck as it flailed weakly, hammering its claws against the floor.

There was movement to his left. Another of the creatures was closing on him, jaws wide. He spun on his heel, raising his knife.

Automatic rifle fire boomed. The monster's head burst open. Its body collapsed, momentum carrying it forwards until it slewed to a halt at Cordero's feet.

He looked up. Ortega stood nearby, rifle barrel smoking. The floor was littered with dead and dying lizards. The air stank of cordite and blood. He could hear a repetitive clicking which took him a moment to realize was the SAW's firing mechanism cycling on an empty drum.

Richards stood by Armstrong's corpse, surrounded by the shattered bodies of more of the lizards. His finger remained clamped around the SAW's trigger and his face was pulled into a rictus grin. Tears streamed down his cheeks.

In the steady beam of Ortega's light, Cordero could see the surviving creatures retreating into the darkness. He could get a better look at them now. They were definitely reptiles, but didn't move like any lizard he had ever seen; they stood upright, heads and tails held erect, and they bobbed up and down as they ran, like birds.

They looked, Cordero thought, like the dinosaur illustrations in the books his mom borrowed from the library when he was a child. He had been fascinated by those colorful depictions of a prehistoric time filled with giants and monsters. They showed a very different world to the smog-choked, sunbaked LA streets outside the window of the room he'd shared with his brothers.

Ortega moved over to Richards and spoke softly to the big man, who lowered the SAW. Cordero scanned the ground for his lost AR. It was nowhere to be seen.

Ortega saw him looking. "Take mine," he said, tossing it to Cordero. "I'll help Richards."

"I don't need help," Richards rumbled. He swatted Ortega's hand from his shoulder. "I can carry him."

"I've got him," Cordero said gently. He slung Ortega's AR and stooped to pick up the commando, feeling a stab of anger towards the man, who had been unconscious throughout the attack. He hefted the dead weight onto his shoulders.

Then he saw that Richards hadn't been talking about the commando. Instead, he was kneeling alongside Armstrong's mutilated body.

"Easy, buddy," Ortega said. "I've got his tags. But we have to leave him here."

Richards rounded on him, face twisted with rage. "We can't leave him here. We have to help him."

Ortega looked pityingly at the corpse. Armstrong's skin was blanched white from blood loss, his eyes open and staring blankly at the ceiling. His torso was open from neck to sternum and his internal organs had been pulled out, lying in bloody coils on the cold steel floor.

"Richards, he's dead. We have to go. Those things could be back at any moment."

As if to emphasize Ortega's words, an animal snarl echoed from the darkness. Ortega swept his light in a wide arc; a dozen sets of eyes glittered around them.

"We have to go *now.*"

Richards allowed himself to be pushed along by Ortega. He moved woodenly, the SAW hanging forgotten in his grip. Ortega flashed a warning glance at Cordero, who nodded his understanding.

They had both seen this before, in the jungles of South America. Soldiers shutting down in the face of horrors they couldn't comprehend. Cordero had seen twenty-year veterans freeze, something snapping within them. Some of them got over it. Many did not.

Cordero's mind kept flashing back to the pages of those books he had read as a kid, cross-legged on the bedroom floor in the spot where the sunlight shone through the window. He felt as though they had stepped into those pages.

But he had a responsibility to get his team to safety. He had already failed Armstrong, walking into an obvious ambush because he hadn't been paying full attention. He wouldn't get sloppy like that again.

Straining under the weight of the commando, Cordero quickly reached a set of bulkhead doors stenciled with the label 'B7'.

Finally, he thought. He placed the commando against the wall then opened the door, stepping through into the lab, rifle at the ready.

It wasn't a lab, he realized. It was some sort of loading facility, probably storage for the main laboratory. Crates of equipment were stacked on bare aluminum shelving. A row of lockers lined one wall, the limp white forms of biohazard suits visible through plexiglass doors. The lights were on, and the room temperature felt normal. Thankfully, the room was empty.

Cordero dragged the commando inside the loading room, before rushing back to the corridor.

Ortega helped Richards down the corridor. Ortega's face was rigid with fear. "I can hear them behind us," he whispered.

Without pausing for thought, Cordero fired a trio of shots past his team. He was rewarded with a shriek of pain, but he counted at least half a dozen of the lizard creatures stalking them in the light of the muzzle flash.

"Let's go!" he roared, as the light faded and the creatures surged forwards. Cordero stepped into the corridor to meet them.

His shout seemed to galvanize Richards, who began to run, Ortega at his side. The pair of them got past Cordero and continued running.

Cordero fired again, backing away to follow them. There were more shrieks. He fired short, controlled bursts; not aiming at anything, just wanting to keep the creatures at bay.

He risked a glance back. He was ten meters from the loading room. Ortega had helped Richards through the door and was in the process of dragging the commando in too.

Something hissed. He fired blind, the sound pounding his bruised ears.

Eight meters. Five. With every step, he fired a burst, praying that he would get to the door before the magazine ran dry.

Click. So much for prayer.

The dinosaur creatures seemed to realize this at the same moment he did. There came a babble of barks, and the sound of multiple clawed feet rushing towards him.

He saw them in the light from the open door of the loading room. Their jaws were open, their claws were raised, and they closed with dizzying speed.

He turned and ran, dropping the empty AR in his haste. Ortega and Richards shouted encouragement from the doorway. He leaned into the sprint, feeling hot breath on the back of his neck. The door was still impossibly far.

And then, he was through, into the room beyond. The door shut solidly behind him. Something heavy crashed into it, snarling.

Cordero slumped to the floor, his breath coming in ragged gasps. His mind spun, trying to comprehend what they had just been through. Armstrong was dead, there were monsters out of some prehistory textbook running round the station. What had happened here?

The clawing at the door slowed, then faded away entirely. Cordero took a deep breath.

"Everyone ok?"

Ortega nodded numbly, staring around at the room. Richards growled a response, which Cordero took as a positive sign. At least he wasn't walking around like a zombie anymore.

He checked the still-unconscious commando. The older man appeared no worse than when they'd found him; there was no fresh blood, no bite or claw marks. He had escaped the attack without a scratch.

"What were those things?" Ortega's voice sounded distant. Cordero gave him a concerned glance. His friend was pale and sweating.

"I can't be sure, but they looked like-"

"Dinosaurs." Richards spoke through gritted teeth. "They were dinosaurs. Utahraptors, I reckon."

"How do you-"

"I used to date a paleontologist from the University of Texas." Richards's confusion had passed, Cordero was glad to see, replaced with a simmering rage. "Learned more about dinosaurs than I ever cared to know. Learned a few other things too." He smirked.

Ortega was shaking his head. "It doesn't make sense. We're in space, man. Space! How would dinosaurs even get into space?"

"I don't know," Richards said grimly. "But I know what I saw."

He pushed himself to his feet, steadying himself by using the SAW like a crutch. He unhooked a fresh drum from his harness and slapped it into the gun.

"And I know what I'm gonna do about it, too."

He stepped towards the door.

Cordero got himself between Richards and the door. "What are you doing?"

"I'm doin' the right thing, Chief. I'm gonna kill those dinosaurs."

"Are you crazy?" Cordero asked. As soon as the words left his mouth, he realized that Richards was. His eyes were wide, showing the whites. Spittle built up at the corners of his mouth. The cords in his neck stood out starkly.

Richards bared his teeth. "Get out of my way, Chief. This needs to happen."

Cordero put his hands on Richards's chest. Richards tried to push past. Cordero pushed back. The bigger man stopped and drew himself up to his full height.

Cordero inhaled deeply. "He's gone, Richards. He's dead."

Richards ran a hand over his scalp. "I know. That's why they need to die, too."

"It won't bring him back."

"It will-"

"It won't bring him back," Cordero repeated. "But we can survive. If we work together."

Richards opened his mouth to retort. Then, he stepped back, shoulders slumped. "Alright."

"Chief." Ortega was kneeling next to a pile of rags. "What was the name of the exec we are looking for?"

"Markovitz," Cordero said. "Why?"

Ortega pulled something from the rags. It was an arm, limp and pale. It had been chewed off at the wrist.

"I think we've found her."

ELEVEN

Elaine Markovitz was dead.

She had been dead for several hours. Something - Cordero didn't like to think about what - had torn apart her rib cage and eaten her internal organs. Her chest gaped open like a shelled clam.

Once it had finished her lungs and heart, whatever had killed Markovitz had started on her limbs. One leg was gone, twisted off at the knee. Her left hand, and the entirety of her right arm, were also missing.

Perversely, her head had been left untouched. The face of a middle-aged woman with stern lines around startlingly blue eyes stared glassily at Cordero from behind the cracked lenses of a pair of designer glasses.

He keyed his comm. "Black, where is Markovitz now?"

It took Black a minute to respond. When he did, it sounded like he was chewing. "Umm, looks like she's moved out of B7. She's headed to something labelled the 'Nexus Chamber' on the station map, whatever that means."

Cordero rubbed his face. From the other side of Markovitz's corpse, Ortega sighed heavily. "She's not in B7 anymore?"

"Nope. Sorry Chief, I should have kept a closer watch and let you know when she moved. Still, at least she's moving around, so I guess that means she's alive, right?"

"You guessed wrong, Black. We're with Markovitz now."

"Oh?" Cordero didn't speak, waiting for the reality of their situation to dawn on Black. "Oh. I take it she's missing her wrist implant then?"

"And her wrists. That body we found when we arrived wasn't the only one to get eaten. And we think we know what's been doing the eating." Cordero told Black what had happened since they'd left the control deck: about the ambush, the dinosaurs, and Armstrong's death.

"None of this makes any sense," Black said, once he had stopped cursing.

"People keep saying that," Ortega said. "Yet here we are."

"I can't believe Armstrong's dead." Black spoke softly, almost to himself. "I always thought that cold bastard could survive anything."

"Yeah, well." Cordero couldn't think of what to say. Armstrong's grizzly death was still fresh in his head. He suppressed the memory of the man's horrified screams. "We need a plan."

"We need to get the fuck off this station." Richards had been standing quietly by the door, resting his forehead against the steel wall. "The exec's dead. Mission over."

"Her wrist implant is still out there, somewhere," Cordero said. He didn't relish the idea of retrieving it from inside whatever had eaten Markovitz, but that was an option. He was just about to say so when the unconscious commando groaned, rolled over, and vomited.

Richards was on the man like a shot. Both of his hands clamped around the man's throat and he started to squeeze. The man gagged, choking on his own vomit. His face began to turn a deep shade of purple.

"No!" Cordero shouldered Richards off the commando, sending him sprawling to the floor. Cordero stepped over the choking man to stand between him and Richards, who was getting to his feet, red with rage.

"That motherfucker tried to kill us!" Richards spat. "He tried-"

"This motherfucker might be the only way to find out what's happening." Cordero held his palms up towards Richards. He sensed Ortega come to stand at his shoulder. "I'm guessing his team caused it. We can find out what we need to know from him. Then we can get the hell out of here."

"My team," the commando croaked. "What happened... my team?"

Cordero squatted on his haunches and faced the man, who had propped himself up on his elbows. His face was still an unhealthy purple, but his breathing was becoming more regular.

"Your team are all dead," Cordero said coldly. "We killed them."

The man sagged back. His head lolled to the side, a trail of blood drooling from his lips. "Damn," he whispered in a voice like sandpaper. Cordero caught the hint of an Appalachian accent over the roughness.

The man looked back at Cordero. "I guess you'll want to kill me now."

"Damn straight." Richards stepped forwards, cracking his knuckles. Cordero stopped him with a glare.

"That depends on how you answer our questions," he said.

The man grinned. There was no warmth or humor in it. Cordero was reminded of a shark. "I've heard that before. Said it myself a few times. Always ended the same way, too, and not well for the one in my position." He extended a scarred, bloody hand. "Still, no harm in being polite. The name's Schaefer."

Cordero let the handshake hang in the air. After a moment, Schaefer lowered it. The grin got wider.

"Tell me, *Schaefer*," Cordero said. "Who do you work for?"

"Now that," Schaefer said, "that would be telling."

Cordero smiled, his jaw tense. He watched Schaefer carefully, unblinking, taking note of every movement. "That's why I'm asking. Don't make me ask again."

Schaefer's grin didn't falter. "I'm under a non-disclosure agreement. You know how those things are. I talk, I get strung up in court."

"You don't talk," Richards snarled, "you get strung up right here. I'll leave you for the dinosaurs to use as a piñata."

Schaefer turned questioning eyes at Cordero. Cordero shrugged. Richards wasn't joking.

"Fine, fine." Schaefer swallowed hard. He raised his eyes to the ceiling. "I work for Miyamoto." He glanced at them, gauging their reaction.

Cordero just nodded. He wasn't surprised. Although the Miyamoto corporation weren't one of Lulworth's fiercest competitors, he had heard that they were making moves into weapons research, Lulworth's main source of income.

"You're here on an industrial espionage job?" Ortega asked.

"Yeah. Miyamoto has a mole on the research team here. They reported back that their work was getting close to finishing. Miyamoto decided they'd rather it didn't get finished at all. So, they sent me and my team to shut things down."

"What was the work?" Richards demanded.

Schaefer's eyes widened fractionally. "You mean, you don't know?"

"Never mind that," Cordero cut in. "What about the crew. Are there any other survivors?"

"No one comes to mind." Schaefer lay back, wincing as the back of his head touched the floor. "Just me and my team, until you good gentlemen arrived."

"How did you know we were coming?" Richards growled.

"We didn't."

"You set an ambush for us."

"Ok, well, we didn't know you were here until you unlocked the doors. Then we assumed that either one of the crew had found their way to control or there was another team on board."

"I thought you said the crew were dead?" Ortega said.

"I mean, I was *presuming* that." Schaefer gestured at Marovitz's corpse. "You've seen what's running around. We thought everybody would be dead by now. When those doors opened, it coulda been a survivor." He glanced at the exec's body again. "Guess not, though."

"Where did all these... *things* come from?"

"You can say it, you know." Schaefer smirked. "They're dinosaurs. Like in the movies."

"Fine, where did these dinosaurs come from?"

"Now that, I do know." Schaefer hauled himself into a sitting position. He leaned back against an overturned desk. "Oh yeah, I had a ringside seat for that."

Cordero leaned in, staring the man dead in the eyes. "Start talking."

They had launched out of Manila earlier that morning, Schaefer said. His team were told to stop the research project with extreme prejudice. That was the extent of their orders. Schaefer had asked about the nature of the research, but their executive liaison had refused to answer.

"Typical corporate bullshit," he shrugged. "You know how it is." The others nodded. It didn't matter who you worked for, executives would always act as though you weren't good enough to lick their boots.

Schaefer's team had entered orbit in an automated stealth shuttle. It was an in-house development at Miyamoto, not yet released commercially. The thing was tiny, barely enough room for Schaefer and his small team, but it had brought them in under the *Buckland's* sensors. They had landed on the hull and cut their way inside the station without being detected.

"We took a detour through the living quarters on our way to the lab complex. Thought we'd have some fun with the crew before the alarm got tripped." Schaefer sneered. "We caught them with their pants down. Literally, in some cases. Most had just finished their shift, were getting ready for bed or to head out for dinner."

Cordero grimaced. He had met men like Schaefer before. Corporations like Lulworth and Miyamoto didn't exactly discourage sadists in their ranks. "Get on with it," he spat.

"We got to where we were headed. Where the mole had told us to go. Where they were working on the Nexus Project."

The Nexus Project. Black had mentioned that Markovitz's wrist implant was showing up in somewhere labelled the 'Nexus Chamber.' That had to be where the experiment had been taking place.

After killing more of the research team, including their mole - "Miyamoto doesn't like to leave loose threads hanging," Schaefer laughed - his team had reached the center of research activity on the *Buckland.*

"The place was filled with all kinds of machinery. I ain't no scientist, so I don't know for sure what I was looking at, but it all looked real complicated, real *expensive* to me."

There had been a raised dais in the center of the chamber, on which a huge freestanding circular arch had stood.

"In the middle of it all was this huge arch thing, like in St Louis. The air inside it looked weird." Schaefer furrowed his brow. "Like smoke or somethin'."

The researchers had taken one look at Schaefer's team and rushed for the doors. Schaefer had tried to stop them, demanding that they shut down the experiment, but his team's blood was up. He hadn't seen who had fired the first shot, but soon everyone was shooting. The panicked researchers had stampeded towards Schaefer's team, into the gunfire. It had been a massacre.

"Then, everything changed." Schaefer turned ashen. He was staring right through Cordero now, transfixed by his memories. "I don't know if they were attracted to the screaming, or the smell of blood, or what. But something big came through that archway."

It had been some sort of dinosaur, from his description. Huge and scaly, with finger length teeth, tree trunk thick hind legs and vestigial forelimbs. It sounded to Cordero like some kind of tyrannosaur. *The king of the lizards,* he remembered.

The beast stepped through the doorway and clamped its massive jaws down on a screaming scientist.

"It shook that poor bastard apart like a dog with a rat," Schaefer said. "Then, everyone started running. Those scientists, my guys, even though I told them to stand and fight. That just made the thing more excited. It was like a fox in a henhouse, killin' everything it could see. Even got a couple of my guys.

"Then another one came through the doorway."

Schaefer and the survivors of his team had turned and ran. They had headed back towards their stealth shuttle but, before they could get out of the labs, the station's security protocols had locked down, trapping them inside with the dinosaurs.

"And that's where we stayed," Schaefer concluded. "Been here for the last few hours. Heard a lot of screaming and roaring in that time, but we hunkered down and kept out of the way. Then you came along and opened the doors for us."

"So you set up an ambush for us," Cordero said.

Schaefer tilted his head. "We had broken onto the station and caused chaos. There was no way you'd be letting us go free."

"No," Cordero said. He stared unblinkingly at Schaefer, eyes cold as ice. "That's true." Cordero stood and stretched, cracking his knuckles. "Ortega, search him. Then tie his hands. We're going to get Black, then we're leaving this station."

Richards narrowed his eyes. His brow wrinkled. "What about the black box?"

"We don't need it." Cordero jabbed a thumb at Schaefer. "He will do."

Schaefer spat a globule of bloody mucus onto the floor. "You're taking me back to be tortured," he said.

"Not tortured," Cordero said. "Interrogated."

"Advanced interrogation techniques, they call it." Richards grinned nastily. "Then they'll prosecute you for damaging company property. If you survive."

Ortega pulled cable from his belt pouch to tie Schaefer's hands. He paused, opened his mouth to speak, then stopped. Collecting his thoughts, he continued:

"We should have Black do a final scan of the station before we go. There might be other survivors on board."

Cordero shrugged nonchalantly, but inside he felt conflicted. Ortega was suggesting the right thing to do, but right now it wasn't part of their job. He didn't want to leave anyone trapped up here with frigging dinosaurs running around, especially knowing that the company would likely blow up the entire facility once they got back.

But he didn't want to lose any more of his men, either.

"They're just going to have to take their chances with the dinosaurs. Tie his hands, Ortega."

Ortega shook his head in disbelief. "We're leaving people here to die, man. Just listen to yourself: you want them to take their chances *with dinosaurs.*"

"He has a point," Schaefer sneered.

"Shut up," Cordero said. "I'm sorry, Juan, but it's my decision. Let it weigh on me. Now come on, we got to get moving."

Ortega shook his head sadly but didn't argue any further. He hooked a hand under Schaefer's arm and hauled him to his feet.

"Steady!" Schaefer cried out in pain, doubling over. Ortega bent over with him, a look of concern on his face.

Schaefer snatched a hand along his boot, quickly and smoothly. He jerked his arm back up in a punching motion.

Ortega grimaced. His grip on Schaefer loosened. Schaefer knocked him to the side and darted towards a side door on the far side of the room.

Cordero grabbed Ortega by the shoulders. "What happened?"

Ortega opened his mouth. A line of blood trickled out. Cordero looked down.

A knife was sticking out of his friend's stomach.

TWELVE

"Juan?"

Ortega fell to his knees, hands wrapped around the knife sticking out of his abdomen. He looked up at Cordero, his face a ghastly grey.

Richards was at his side in an instant. "Leave it, leave it," he muttered, clamping a hand over the wound. He took the medi pack from Ortega's belt and pulled out a roll of pressure bandages.

Ortega winced as Richards gripped the hilt of the blade. His eyes met Cordero's.

"Go get that bastard, Mike."

Cordero stepped forwards. Stopped. "But-"

"I got this." Richards was calm, focused. "We need Schaefer. Go."

"We need-"

"Ortega's alright. The knife didn't hit anything major." Richards didn't even look up. "I got this, Chief. Go."

Cordero unholstered the pistol he'd taken from one of the commandos and offered it to Ortega. "Take this."

"What about you?"

"You think I'll need a weapon when I catch that fucker?"

Ortega took the gun, smearing bright blood on the grip. "Thanks, Mike. Now go. I'll be fine."

Ortega pushed him away and he ran in the same direction as Schaefer, trying to ignore how weak his friend's shove had been.

The side door remained open, leading into a darkened room. He sprinted straight through; if Schaefer were waiting in ambush, he wanted the element of surprise on his side.

He crashed straight into a stack of plastic-coated crates. There was no ambush. Cordero found himself surrounded by aluminum racking that loomed over him, the shelves an untidy jumble of complex-looking scientific equipment that he didn't recognize, much of it damaged, the rest unopened.

Despite the darkness, he could see the walls on either side of him; the room was narrow with a high ceiling, presumably to accommodate the stacks of equipment. Shadowed alcoves lined each wall.

Waiting a beat for his eyes to adjust to the darkness, he moved down the center of the room. He placed his feet carefully, avoiding pieces of abandoned equipment, moving with a silence borne of years of experience.

A sound came from up ahead; a soft scratching, fabric sliding over a rough surface.

Cordero stopped moving, stopped breathing. The sound came again.

Then it stopped. He strained his ears for the slightest noise. He could hear something, very faintly. It sounded like...

Breathing.

Someone was pressed up to the wall, trying to keep quiet.

Got you, he thought, and began to inch towards the sound.

A mechanical grinding noise tore open the silence. Light stabbed into the room.

Cordero ducked behind a crate. On the far side of the room, a large circular door was slowly opening. It looked to Cordero like an airlock door, and he felt the cold hand of fear clutch his heart for a moment, expecting to find himself sucked out into space.

But there was another chamber beyond. As the door opened wider, the light leaching out illuminated a sign on the wall next to it: Purification Chamber.

That explains why they'd build it like an airlock, he thought. *The room is airtight.*

The light revealed something else, too. The figure of a tall man with short white hair, hunched over an activation panel on the wall.

"Schaefer!"

Cordero's control slipped. Before he realized what he was doing, he had leapt out from behind the crate and was charging towards the door. He caught his foot on something hard and stumbled, but his momentum - and his rage - kept him moving.

Schaefer looked up, alarm on his face, to see a hulking figure rushing out of the darkness towards him. He abandoned the panel and darted into the next chamber.

As he got closer, Cordero could see the gleaming chamber through the airlock door. There was another panel in the chamber, the twin of the one outside; Schaefer staggered over to it and hammered on the buttons.

The door stopped opening, growled, then began to close. Cordero gritted his teeth and ran as fast as he could. There were just a few feet remaining between the descending door and the floor. Cordero flung himself into a slide, straightening his body as he leapt.

The door grazed the back of his legs, but he was through. He sprang to his feet in front of Schaefer, bouncing into an uppercut.

His fist connected with Schaefer's chin. The other man's head snapped back, blood spraying from his mouth across an instructional sign behind him. He fell against the wall, dazed.

Cordero didn't give him time to recover. He took two quick steps forward and scythed a kick at Schaefer's head. Schaefer brought his arm up at the last moment to catch the blow, which sent him rolling to one side.

Cordero felt himself lose balance. His leg extended, he couldn't react as Schaefer swept him from his feet with a kick. He fell hard on his side.

Schaefer was on him like a starving dog, fingers jabbing at Cordero's eyes. Cordero turned his head to one side and brought his knees up, catching Schaefer under the abdomen. He kicked out, sending Schaefer staggering backwards.

Cordero jumped up, wiping sweat from his eyes. Schaefer had another knife in his hands. Instantly, Cordero closed, faking to the left before hammering a solid roundhouse to the right side of Schaefer's head.

Schaefer stumbled to one side, slashing his blade wildly to keep Cordero at bay. "Don't make me stick you like I did your friend," he burbled through a mouthful of blood.

"You're welcome to try," Cordero said, watching Schaefer like a hawk.

Schaefer lunged for him, swinging the knife down in an arc. Cordero caught his wrist and twisted hard. Schaefer shrieked, the knife falling from his hand, and brought up a knee into Cordero's crotch.

The air left Cordero's lungs in a rush. Fire roared from his groin to his stomach. He gritted his teeth through the pain. Through tears, he threw a blind flurry of jabs and crosses, feeling them connect.

He took a deep breath, quenching the pain in his balls. Schaefer was staggering backwards, blood streaming from his flattened nose. He fell, sticking out an arm to stop himself. His hand caught the activation panel, and the door began to open.

There was a rumble from behind Cordero. The other airlock was opening too. Cordero risked a glance at the bloodied sign on the wall. Nexus Chamber and Cryogenic Chamber, it declared.

The Nexus Chamber was in the next room. The location of the experiment that had unleashed the dinosaurs on the station.

And the door was opening.

Schaefer tried to move past him, towards the knife. Cordero stepped into his way. He shook his head. "Don't even try it."

Schaefer glanced at the knife, then back to Cordero, then to the now-open airlock door.

"Don't try that, either." Cordero put one boot on the knife. "You're coming back with me."

"No way, pal. That's not happening." Schaefer edged sideways. "I'm not being dragged back to Earth to die."

"Fine." Cordero shrugged. "You can die here."

A bloody grin split Schaefer's face open like a wound. He spread his arms wide. "You keep on trying. And I'm still alive."

Cordero pounced, going from still to a blur in an instant. Schaefer was just as quick, though. Cordero's fingers grazed Schaefer's fatigues as he slipped away. He twisted, grasping after him, but Schaefer was gone out of the door.

Cordero ran after him, snatching up the abandoned knife as he went.

He found himself in a wide, circular room, on a metal walkway that ran around the perimeter. A series of ramps led down from the walkway to a lower floor.

In the center of the room, an enormous archway rose from floor to ceiling. It was near twenty meters tall and roughly circular in shape, made of a darkened metal that he didn't recognize, that glittered in the low light. Thick cabling snaked from the shadows beneath the walkway to wrap around the base of the arch.

Cordero leaned over the railing. The floor below was covered in strange machinery. Here and there, broken bodies lay askew.

The space inside the arch seemed to shimmer, like oil on water. Cordero squinted. Through the haze, he could make out shapes in the wavering air. Trees, tall and top-heavy, wavering in an unfelt breeze. Beyond them rose a range of jagged mountains. Bat winged creatures soared in the sky.

But that couldn't be real. Could it?

He stepped along the walkway, gaze fixed on the center of the arch. Was this what Schaefer had mentioned, some sort of portal through which the dinosaurs had come onboard the *Buckland?*

As he passed a console displaying an ever-changing readout of graphs and charts, he heard something else. Not the rustling of fabric this time.

This was the absence of sound. The too quiet of someone trying to be silent, waiting.

Cordero tensed.

The console exploded with a shriek. Fragments of glass and plastic filled the air. Cordero ducked as the echoes of a gunshot ricocheted around the cavernous room.

He waited for a count of five, then leaned out from the side of his hiding place, trying to minimize his profile.

Next to the portal, Schaefer stood over the chewed corpse of one of his commandos. He held a smoking pistol in one hand.

"Well, well, well. Looks like the tables have turned." Schaefer fired another shot, forcing Cordero to duck back behind the console. A bullet pinged off the wall.

He looked around. The closest escape was the airlock, and there was no cover between him and it. Schaefer could empty half a clip into him before he reached it.

"I'm guessing, from the fact you ain't shooting back, that you didn't bring a gun with you?" Schaefer's mocking voice drifted from across the room. "Hell, boy, I even told you that some of my team died in the Nexus Chamber. Did you think I was running away from you? Nah, I was running towards the guns."

Cordero risked another glance. Schaefer was staring straight at his hiding place. A slow smile spread across the scarred commando's face as he walked towards Cordero.

"Now you just stay right where you are, and I promise to make this quick-"

A bloodcurdling roar drowned Schaefer out. Cordero involuntarily clamped his hands over his ears. Schaefer looked around wildly, the pistol extended.

An enormous crocodilian head burst through the portal and roared again. Schaefer spun to face it, screaming something that Cordero couldn't make out.

The monster - it was a tyrannosaurus, Cordero realized, or something like it - lunged at Schaefer, faster than something so huge should have been able to move. Schaefer tried to dive aside, but the giant's jaws clamped around his torso.

Schaefer screamed as dagger-like teeth sunk into his flesh. Thick blood burst from his mouth as the jaws closed, his scream turning into a gurgle.

Schaefer began to punch at the tyrannosaurus's snout. But the beast barely noticed; it snorted in irritation, then it shook Schaefer like a rag doll. His high-pitched scream was horrifying, pure pain. His body came apart at the seams. Blood splattered in a gory rain as arteries tore open in his legs and neck, spattering the floor with deep red puddles.

Cordero crouched, frozen, like a rabbit that's spotted a coyote, he realized. The door was meters away. He could be gone in seconds. But his muscles refused to move.

He could only watch in horror as the tyrannosaurus tilted back its head and swallowed the dying Schaefer whole. He looked on as the wriggling lump tracked down the beast's throat.

The tyrannosaurus sniffed the air, nostrils flaring. It looked around, black eyes tiny in the giant's head.

Then, the tyrannosaurus emerged from the portal like an enormous crocodile crawling from a calm river. It scanned the chamber with a sweep of its blunt head, still sniffing. The creature was enormous; forty feet from snout to the tip of its tail. Its flesh was mottled purple brown. It looks like Barney, from when I was a kid, Cordero thought crazily.

The monster ducked its head and nuzzled at the remains of the commando that Schaefer had taken the pistol from.

Move, Cordero screamed to himself. With an effort of will, he took a single shuffling step backwards.

The tyrannosaurus looked up, directly at where Cordero was hiding. Its eyes gleamed.

Primal fear sent a shock through his spine. Adrenaline flooded his system. He bound to his feet and sprinted for the airlock door.

There was a bloodcurdling roar behind him, followed by a series of hollow booms as the tyrannosaurus spotted him and took up the chase. He dove into the open airlock, rolling onto his back as he landed. Would the walkway even be able to withstand the monster's weight?

He got his answer immediately. The tyrannosaurus bounded up from the lower floor in a single powerful leap. It slammed into the walkway, which bent beneath its weight, but held.

Cordero scrabbled backwards as the tyrannosaurus thrust its head through the doorway, its jaws snapping inches from his face. It began to claw itself into the airlock, its vestigial forelimbs gripping tightly to the floor.

"Fuck you, Barney!" Cordero screamed, his voice sounding high and alien to his ears. He kicked out, boots connecting with the tyrannosaurus's snout.

The beast snorted. Pushing himself off its nose, Cordero scrambled to his feet and ran into the storage room. The darkness swallowed him like a blanket.

He ran blindly, seeking the door that he knew was just ahead, somewhere in the darkness. A door that the tyrannosaurus couldn't fit through.

He hit his ankle hard on something and was sent flying. He landed hard on his hands, the shock reverberating up his arms.

The light from the airlock suddenly vanished. Cordero looked back.

The tyrannosaurus was forcing its way through the airlock and into the storeroom. It snorted, shaking its head, slamming against the wall. The entire room shook with the force of the impact, causing the tall shelving to sway sickeningly and sending a rain of scientific equipment smashing around Cordero. He dropped to the floor, and covered his head.

An ominous creak juddered through the air. Then, the shriek of tearing metal rent the darkness.

One of the shelving units smashed to the floor with a thunderous crash.

Cordero looked up. Through the gloom and the haze of atomized glass, he saw that the racking had fallen across the center of the room, blocking his path.

The walls shook again. He heard an ominous scraping sound. The tyrannosaurus had squeezed itself through the airlock and stood tall in the storage room. It blinked in the darkness, mouth open as it tasted the air. Its nostrils flexed, seeking his scent.

Cordero ducked behind a shattered packing crate. He felt panic rising in his chest, his breath coming in fast, shallow gasps. With an effort of will, he wrestled back control of his nerves.

Now was not the time to panic. Now was the time to look for a way out of here.

The shelves had crashed together to form a jagged wall. He couldn't see a way through. He could climb it, given time, but not quickly enough to avoid the tyrannosaurus.

He squinted into the darkness, looking to see if there was a way around the sides of the room. Falling debris seemed to have blocked every route through. He was at a dead end; the only way out was to go back towards the airlock and follow the wall around. Right past Barney.

He briefly considered trying to force a gap through some of the surviving shelves, to reach one of the aisles alongside, but they were packed with heavy equipment. Moving those would make too much noise, drawing the tyrannosaurus's attention. The dinosaur appeared to be struggling to see in the low light, but Cordero wasn't going to gamble his life that it couldn't hunt by sound.

No, there was only one way out. He had to kill the tyrannosaurus.

He checked his harness. The knife was gone. He must have dropped it back in the Nexus Chamber. That made things trickier.

Trying to kill a tyrannosaurus rex with my bare hands. It won't be a clean death, but it sure is bad ass.

He wished there were someone around to see it.

A clatter came from inside the airlock. It sounded like something light and plastic bouncing against the wall.

The tyrannosaurus turned its head towards the sound. The beast's eyes narrowed. It growled suspiciously, sounding like the rumble of thunder.

Cordero caught a blur of movement from the corner of his eye. It looked like a radio handset. It flew out of the shadows to sail past the tyrannosaurus.

The tyrannosaurus caught the motion too; it snapped lazily at the handset as it passed, turning its head to follow it.

The handset shattered on the airlock floor with a crackle of static. The tyrannosaurus stepped towards the sound, ducking under the door into the airlock.

Cordero tensed, ready to run. This looked like his only chance to escape. He had no idea who was throwing the handsets, but he would rather face them than a tyrannosaurus.

The tyrannosaurus had retreated almost completely into the airlock. Only its tail protruded from the chamber.

Cordero began to creep forward slowly, wanting to take advantage of the obscuring darkness as long as possible.

The tyrannosaurus turned, looking back into the storage room, pulling its thick tail fully inside the airlock.

Cordero stood. He had barely taken his first step when a figure rushed towards the airlock. The tyrannosaurus spotted them and roared in anger, but the figure was already at the airlock control panel. The doors began to close. The tyrannosaurus turned, its bulk making this difficult. It snarled and snapped, finally managing to turn itself fully around.

The airlock door thudded shut.

THIRTEEN

"You can come out now."

The voice was well-spoken, cultured, and feminine. They sounded calm, if a little out of breath.

Cordero hesitated. The adrenaline that had been surging through him since Schaefer had stabbed Ortega was beginning to ebb away, leaving exhaustion in its place.

It was a familiar feeling, especially from his time in Recon, though he'd never experienced anything as mind-numbingly terrifying as the last few hours. Once the danger had passed, the body demanded a price.

But he had no idea if the danger had passed yet. For all he knew, this stranger was armed and ready to kill.

"I'm not going to hurt you," the voice said, as though reading his thoughts. "I just want to get off this station."

Time to take a leap of faith, Cordero decided. He had to get back to what was left of his team.

He stepped out of the darkness.

"Hi." It was a woman. She was short and slender, her expression serious. Her lab coat was stained with oil, dirt, and blood. Long dark hair was tied back in a sensible ponytail.

"Hi." Cordero nodded reservedly.

"Looks like you've had a bad day." The woman's smile was friendly. She extended a hand. "I'm Dr Conroy. But just call me Shea."

"Mike Cordero." He shook her hand gingerly, dizzy with the sudden change of circumstances. The greeting was so ordinary and yet, moments ago, he had been faced with death by tyrannosaurus. "I'm with a Lulworth Rapid Orbital Response team."

"Nice to meet you, Mike." Shea extracted her hand back from Cordero's confused grip. "Where's the rest of the ROR team?"

Cordero pointed towards the door. "We ran into some trouble. We're leaving now though."

"Can you take me with you?"

Cordero nodded. "Of course."

"Good." She let out a sigh of relief.

Cordero tapped the airlock door. A loud thumping came in response, telling him that the tyrannosaurus still lurked on the other side. "Closing that door was a smart move, Shea. You really saved my ass."

"I saved *both* our asses," Shea countered. "I thought I'd found myself a nice safe spot to wait out this disaster, then you and that other maniac come charging through and let a tyrannosaurus in!" She looked around, concern on her face. "Where's the man you were following?"

Cordero grimaced. "He... well, first, he wasn't a good guy."

Shea nodded. "He was one of the ones who attacked us." She looked away, swallowing slowly. "He killed a lot of people."

"Yeah. He was a real piece of shit."

"Where is he?"

"Barney got him."

"Who?"

"The tyrannosaurus."

"Oh." Cordero wasn't expecting the look of relief on her face. "They were worse than the dinosaurs, you know? They killed people for fun."

"I know."

Shea's eyes glistened. Cordero gritted his teeth, uncomfortable. He was ex-special forces, a space faring commando. He was never sure how to deal with others' emotions.

He wished Ortega were here; his friend was much more comfortable comforting others. It was a skill that Cordero had never really mastered.

Instead, he changed the subject. "Why are there dinosaurs on the *Buckland*?"

Shea's demeanor changed at the question. She stood straighter, as though speaking to a packed lecture hall. "Did the company tell you what we were doing up here, before they sent you?"

"Not really. I just know what's in the *Buckland's* file. Weapons research, right?"

"Right." Shea rolled her eyes. "Makes sense that the company would designate us as weapons research. We started out looking for alternate forms of transport."

Cordero frowned. "Dinosaurs?"

Shea laughed. "Not our primary goal, no. Do you know anything about temporal synchronicity? Localized space-time tearing?"

"I failed high school physics. Twice."

Shea laughed. A deep smoker's laugh, in contrast to her stature. "I'll take that as a no, then." She looked Cordero up and down. "Lulworth really will just launch anyone into space, won't they? No offence."

"None taken." Cordero grinned at her. "They're more worried about making sure we know which end of the gun goes boom."

"Typical corp." Shea brushed a stray hair out of her eyes. "They asked us to find a way to open localized wormholes."

"Wormholes? As in, portals?" Cordero may have failed physics, but he had seen his fair share of science fiction movies.

Shea looked like she was about to say something else, but then thought better of it. "Basically, yes. We were working on ways to open portals that allowed instantaneous transport from one place to another."

"Did it work?"

"Oh yes, we did it. We were able to create gamma to sigma class apertures that allowed transport from one side of the station to the other."

"From one side of the station to the other? That's barely two kilometers."

Shea's brow creased. "Range was an issue. It's what we were working on when we were attacked."

"And that led to dinosaurs running around?"

"Not exactly. Our latest attempts solved the spatial problem but created a temporal problem. Which I'm fairly certain was due to us misunderstanding some fundamental principles of quantum oscillation, that I can account for next time we try..."

Cordero held up a hand. "Let's skip the lessons learnt. Your fix screwed up something else."

Shea sighed. "We could open a portal on Earth from here, but not in the present."

Cordero rubbed his chin. "You opened a doorway to the past."

"It opened *where* we wanted it to," Shea continued. "We aimed for the North American badlands - there's a company testing station there, so we knew it was a safe place - but the aperture opened approximately seventy million years into the past."

"Right, right." A slow smile spread across Cordero's face. "And then, dinosaurs."

"Once we realized what had happened, we started to shut the experiment down. But then those gunmen arrived, and..." She tailed off.

"It's ok," Cordero said. "I saw what happened next."

She grasped Cordero's arm suddenly. "I've been hiding in here ever since. When the screaming stopped, I thought it was safe to go back, to shut down the portal. But then you arrived."

"Don't worry about it." Cordero put a hand on hers. "You're safe now." That wasn't true, but the last thing he needed was for her to panic. "We can leave."

Shea wasn't listening. Her stare drifted to the airlock. "Do you think the rex is gone?" she said. "If you can get me to the portal, I can shut it down."

"No," Cordero said firmly. "We're leaving. Now. Once we regroup with my team, I'll have Mac prep the *Silverback* for launch. Then, we're gone."

"What's the *Silverback?*" Shea asked.

"It's our ticket off of this station," Cordero said.

FOURTEEN

MacTiernan leaned back in the pilot seat, his boots up on the shuttle's control panel, and inhaled deeply on his cigar. His toe tapped in time to the beat of the music blasting through the cockpit's speakers. Czar Lugaflow, the *creme de la creme* of Uganda's thriving trip hop scene. It was lo fi, lo tech, full of bone-shuddering beats. Just the sort of thing MacTiernan needed to help him relax while the rest of the team were off ship.

He checked the mission timer. It had been a couple of hours since he'd heard anything from Cordero. That was unusual; his role was to get the team to the mission site, and, with most ROR teams, he would hear nothing until it was time to leave. But Cordero always insisted on keeping him updated. He had told him not to bother, but Cordero had insisted. His silence now left McTernan feeling unnerved.

Something caught his attention. Something was off with the music, a stray note or odd sound.

There. It happened again.

"Music. Off," he said. The speakers shut off instantly, leaving MacTiernan feeling alone and exposed in a quiet, smoky cockpit.

The sound came again. It was a fast, staccato rattle. A *tap-tap-tap*. Then, it stopped.

He stood and looked out of the windscreen, sure that it had come from outside the shuttle. There was nothing out there, just the empty docking chamber.

MacTiernan shook his head. He had spent too much time sat alone on the shuttle. He must have been imagining things.

The tapping came again. Louder this time.

"Alright, guess I'm not imagining things." The sound of his voice was oddly soothing. Damn, but he was spooked.

"Activate external cameras," he said. The speakers gave an answering chime, letting him know that the *Silverback's* system had picked up the command.

Across the control panel, a trio of monitors flickered to life. Each displayed a view on the exterior of the shuttle: one from the underside, the other the roof and the last from the tail. MacTiernan checked them all carefully, then checked them again. Nothing.

Damn, he had been hoping for something obvious. A loose panel, maybe, or malfunctioning tail flap; the sort of thing that could be repaired with a quick spacewalk before the team got back.

The rattling came again. It sounded like it was coming from outside.

Then it hit him. It could be the sound of the others returning. Perhaps something had happened, something that had stopped Cordero getting in touch. A fault with the comms system.

Maybe there were casualties.

He opened the cockpit door and grabbed the medi pack. He paused for a moment when his gaze fell across the shotgun. It might make him feel better to have it in his hands while he was out there.

No, better not. He didn't want to face the jokes and questions of the others.

He went through into the crew cabin and keyed open the exterior door. As he did, he heard another sound. It was a hollow coughing, almost like a bark.

He stopped, finger hovering over the door control panel. But the sound didn't come again.

It could be one of the team, he thought. They might have picked up some virus. Great, he'd have to make sure they stayed in the crew cabin. There was no way he would be spending the next few weeks in quarantine once they got back; he had leave coming up.

MacTiernan stepped out into the umbilical. The silence was deafening. He sniffed; there was an odd smell out here, dry and musky.

"Cordero?" He called. "Richards?"

His voice echoed down the corridor. He waited by the *Silverback's* door and counted to ten, listening.

Nothing.

"Great." He walked further down the umbilical, and stepped into the docking platform. His eyes took a moment to adjust to the low lighting. Shadows seemed to move around him. The musky smell was stronger here, almost unbearably so.

He wished he had brought the shotgun.

He had just decided to go back and get it when something moved to his right. He spun.

In the center of the docking platform, a loading truck lay on its side. A smashed crate lay a couple of meters away, the lid open, a mess of putrefying fruit spilling out.

As MacTiernan watched, a rotting orange rolled out of the crate, along the floor, then stopped.

That must have been what he'd seen moving. And it could have been the source of the rattling sound, too.

MacTiernan laughed at his own nervousness. "Get it together, man," he said to the empty room, walking back to the umbilical. "You're jumping at fruit now."

The coughing sound came from behind him. He glanced over his shoulder.

An enormous lizard was rushing across the platform towards him. Its mouth was open in a snarl, revealing rows of hooked teeth. The long talons on the ends of its limbs gleamed in the low lighting.

MacTiernan screamed, an involuntary sound of terror. In just a few seconds the lizard had almost closed the gap.

He sprinted to the unbiblical. Almost instantly, he was sweating. Being a shuttle pilot meant he wasn't required to take the physical tests the company required from their response teams - something he was regretting now. He could feel the creature's hot fetid breath on the back of his neck.

The shotgun, the shotgun, he repeated, like a mantra. *Got to get the shotgun.*

He barreled into the *Silverback's* crew cabin, straight into the cockpit. He snatched the old shotgun off its rack on the wall. In the same moment, he realized his mistake.

He hadn't shut the doors behind him.

The musky smell was back, as strong as it had been on the docking platform.

He spun back to face the crew cabin. The lizard was there. It snarled, and leapt.

MacTiernan shrieked, throwing his hands up in front of his face.

The creature hit him like a ton of bricks. Its weight knocked him from his feet. He staggered backwards into the pilot's cabin, the lizard on top of him, snapping and snarling. He screamed, trying to push it away. Belatedly, he realized that the shotgun was still in his hands, held across his front like a crossbar.

It saved his life. The monster lunged for his throat. Instead, it bit down on the gun barrel, teeth sinking into the metal. It snapped its head back, tearing the shotgun from his hands.

Full of terror, MacTiernan kicked out. He hit the creature in the rib cage, knocking it back into the crew compartment.

MacTiernan reached behind him, frantically seeking the control deck, his eyes fixed on the lizard as it scrabbled to its feet. He found the door controls and jabbed at them.

The doors closed quickly. But the monster was just as quick, though not fast enough. It was halfway through the doors when they slammed down on its chest.

The beast howled in agony. It writhed, trapped between the doors.

The coughing sound came again. Through the partially open doors, MacTiernan saw two more of the creatures enter the shuttle.

There was a searing pain in his left foot. While he was distracted, the monster between the doors had clamped its jaws down around his boot. He screamed in pain, kicking at its head with his other foot.

His kick connected hard, but the beast tenaciously held on. He lined up his next kick when, glancing up, he saw another lizard trying to force its way through the gap in the door.

Screaming wordlessly now, MacTiernan fired a trio of rapid kicks at the creature holding onto his boot. One, two, three shots connected, and it loosened its grip.

MacTiernan dragged himself backwards, out of the reach of the monsters.

There was a metallic squeal. MacTiernan's eyes widened.

"Oh no, no, no, no, no."

The second lizard had joined the first. Together, they were gradually forcing the doors open. The trapped creature howled in agony as the pressure around its chest lessened, grinding the ribs together.

It was only a matter of time before they forced their way into the cockpit. He had to act, now.

MacTiernan climbed to his feet and slapped a hand down on the shuttle's ignition. The *Silverback's* engines had always been fast to heat up, and she didn't let him down this time. They roared instantly to life, sending juddering shocks through the shuttle.

The monsters stopped trying to force open the doors and looked around for the source of the sound, hissing in alarm. Keeping one eye on them, MacTiernan slid into the pilot's seat and increased the throttle. The engines screamed and the vibrations became almost painful, risking damage to the shuttle as it strained against the grip of the docking clamps.

Despite their alarm, the monsters didn't scatter as he hoped they would. Instead, the noise and motion galvanized them into greater action. They barked and roared, trying to squeeze themselves through the gap between the doors.

There was another option, though it was a risk. MacTiernan strapped into the pilot's seat. He reached under the control panel, removed the oxygen mask from its storage compartment and attached it to his face.

He turned to look at the monsters.

"Eat this, you sons of bitches."

MacTiernan deactivated the docking clamps. The *Silverback* leapt forwards, free from its constraints. The shuttle accelerated with bone-crushing force, straight at the dock's internal wall. MacTiernan yanked the control stick hard to the right, dropping the throttle and hitting the retros, sending the shuttle into a harsh turn that left a black line seared in its wake as its exhausts came within meters of the wall.

MacTiernan turned the *Silverback* towards open space. Bracing himself against the cold and pressure loss, he levelled the shuttle out and pushed the throttle to its maximum.

The *Silverback* leapt out into open space.

With a hollow boom, the oxygen in the shuttle exploded out of the open exterior door. MacTiernan screamed as his eardrums burst. He rose from his seat as the shuttle left the *Buckland's* gravity field, the seat straps digging into his shoulders as they held him in place.

One of the lizards, startled to find itself floating in midair, lost its grip on the door. It was instantly yanked towards the exterior door, smashing against the door with a bone-shattering crunch, before tumbling out into space.

The creature pinned between the doors shrieked as it was sucked out of the shuttle to join its companion, leaving behind shreds of skin and bone, and a cloud of blood. It knocked into the final creature as it passed, sending it crashing against the wall.

The obstacle removed, the cockpit doors finally began to close. They must have been damaged, though; halfway to closing, they reversed direction and opened all the way.

Cursing, MacTiernan hit a switch to close the exterior doors. He breathed a heavy sigh of relief into the oxygen mask, feeling warm prickles along his arm as the *Silverback's* life support systems began to re-establish a comfortable interior atmosphere.

He mopped the frozen perspiration from his brow, turning the *Silverback* around, back to the station.

A coughing bark came from behind. His blood turned to ice in his veins.

Slowly, he turned.

Halfway up the back wall of the crew compartment, one of the lizard creatures hung like an enormous bat. It stared at him hungrily.

"Oh shit."

MacTiernan twisted in his chair, reaching for the control panel.

The monster launched itself from the wall like a rocket, slamming into MacTiernan's midsection.

He screamed in hot agony as razor sharp talons tore into his stomach. Gouts of blood - so much blood - filled the air around him. He felt a dozen knives stabbing into his neck; the creature had him in its jaws.

The last thing he saw was the *Buckland* growing larger in the windscreen as the shuttle accelerated towards it.

FIFTEEN

Black was through with the *Buckland's* security systems. Nothing was working as it was supposed to and he was ready to give up trying to retrieve the black box.

There were telltale traces of someone having wreaked deliberate havoc on the station's systems, but he couldn't track exactly what they had done; the only success he'd had was locating where they'd gotten access, a terminal in the staff cabins. He had also found anomalous power readings coming from the station's hull near a water store. The terminal, he had noticed, lay between the labs and the unusual hull reading.

Black stubbed out his cigarette, readying himself to tackle the mainframe one more time, when everything jolted sideways.

He was flung to the floor, smashing his head against the side of a desk.

Feeling woozy, he tried to stand, but fell again. The entire room still seemed to be shaking violently. He must have hit his head worse than he thought. Either that, or something was seriously wrong with the *Buckland.*

Black had grown up in the Japanese Protectorate. He remembered being woken one morning by his room shaking. He had run into his parent's room screaming and his dad, still half-asleep, had reassured him that it was a gentle earthquake.

What was happening now was far from gentle. He tried to stand again but was thrown to his knees. Desks that had been secured to the floor moments before tore free and began to slide around the room, shedding broken glass and shattered plastic.

"Black." His radio was crackling in his ear. "Black, come in!"

"Cordero?" He pressed himself to the floor and laced his fingers over his head, praying for everything to stop shaking.

"You ok?"

"Um." The room still seemed to be spinning, but he was able to keep his balance when he stood. "Yeah, I think so. Took a knock to the head but otherwise I'm fine."

"Thank God. Do you know what just happened?"

That was a good question. Black stumbled over to the central terminal and pulled up a system report.

"This looks bad, Chief."

A heavy sigh crackled down the comm. "Tell me all about it."

Black had no idea where to begin. "Well, it looks like something hit us, real hard and real fast. The docking module is gone, and the two sections on either side of it are venting oxygen. Looks like their emergency bulkheads have failed."

"Christ." Cordero still sounded calm, somehow. "Any sign of the *Silverback?* Or MacTiernan?"

"Nothing. They're just... gone. The docking system detected a departure shortly before - before whatever just happened. Got to assume it was the *Silverback.*"

"Something must have gotten to Mac," Cordero said under his breath. "What else?"

Black exhaled heavily. "Well, there are system failure reports all over the station. The life support is out in some areas. Artificial gravity is coming on and off in some sections. Security is shot, door locks are out. And I'm seeing reports of multiple fires and some weird energy spikes. But that's not the worst of it."

"There's worse?"

"'Fraid so." Black swallowed. His throat was dry and his head throbbed. He would kill for a cup of cold water about now. "Whatever hit the station knocked it out of its orbit. We're going down, Chief."

There was a muffled curse on the other end of the link. "How long until we enter atmosphere?"

Black booted up the *Buckland's* navigation system and ran some predictive algorithms. "Two hours, give or take."

More quiet. Black thought he heard Cordero talking to someone else, off mike. He leaned back in the chair and closed his eyes, waiting for the throbbing in his skull to subside. He could hear his pulse thundering in his ears. It sounded almost like giant footsteps.

"Black?"

He blinked. "Yes, Chief?"

"You still there?"

"Yep," he said, though he wasn't sure.

"Good man. We need you to check something for us, ok? We think the other team arrived on some sort of stealth shuttle. It probably wouldn't have been picked up by the station's scanners, but it's likely to have connected to the *Buckland's* systems somewhere. They will have wanted a direct link to siphon whatever data they could."

"Makes sense, Chief." Remote access would have been far too obvious, and easily blocked if detected. "You want me to look for anything out of place?"

"You got it. Have you seen anything?"

Black rubbed his eyes. He suddenly felt incredibly weary. "Those commandos did a real number on the system. And it wasn't standard to begin with. It'll be hard to separate the stuff the crew did themselves from what the shuttle's doing."

But even as he spoke, he realized that he already knew the answer. The anomalous power reading he had spotted earlier, on the hull near the crew compartment.

He checked the system logs; whatever was draining power produced no output...

"Chief, I know where it is." He pulled up the station schematics and uploaded the location of the reading onto a portable tablet on the desk. "I'll put it on a map and meet you at the labs."

"Black, wait." Black stopped, already out of the chair. "Before you leave, we need you to check for any signs of life across the station."

"Give me five." Black sat back down and commanded the *Buckland's* sensors to scan for life signs. There were a few dark areas where the station's scanners had been inoperable, but most of the area around the control deck and the labs still gave a reading. He wasn't sure what Cordero hoped to find, though. They had already checked for life signs when they'd reached the control deck and had only found a handful, which had likely been the Miyamoto commandos and the dinosaurs they had already encountered.

What he saw made him gasp.

"What's up?"

"We got life signs, Chief. Lots of them. Some big ones, too." He stood, shouldering his AR. "And they're heading my way."

Cordero said something in reply, but Black wasn't paying attention. Instead, he was listening to the thundering of his pulse. A thundering that sounded a lot like footsteps.

It was getting louder.

SIXTEEN

Cordero looked round the corner towards the control deck entrance, then ducked back.

"Anything?" Richards asked.

"The door's open," Cordero said. "It looks busted."

"Something might have gotten in." Shea peered round the hunched form of Ortega.

"You think?" Richards sneered, casting a look of displeasure at the scientist. He had been unhappy with Shea joining them from the moment she and Cordero had arrived back in the storage room.

"Hey man, go easy." Unlike Richards, Ortega had taken a liking to Shea. The feeling seemed mutual; she had supported him on the journey back to the control deck. He leaned on her now, for support.

Cordero was worried for Ortega; his friend's skin was pale and clammy, and his breath was coming in shallow gasps. The bandages wrapped around his abdomen were stained pink with blood. He needed proper medical attention, fast.

Cordero looked back around the corner. Whatever had broken open the control deck doors had hit them hard. There were claw marks dug into the metal. Whatever had made them was big, bigger than the raptors.

He tried to raise Black on the radio again. Still nothing.

It was quiet. If some enormous dinosaur had gotten into the control deck, Cordero would expect to have heard it by now. Animals that large couldn't move without making some noise. But there was nothing except deathly silence.

There was only one way to find out what had happened to Black.

"Come on," he said to Richards. The big man nodded and hefted the SAW. Ortega started to follow, but Cordero stopped him.

"You need to stay with Shea." Ortega started to protest, but Cordero cut him off. He put an arm around Ortega's shoulder and leaned in close to whisper, "She's a civilian. I can't risk taking her with me. But I can't leave her undefended either."

Ortega agreed, as Cordero knew he would. He also knew that Shea would look out for him too.

Cordero entered the control deck first, ahead of Richards. It looked like a tornado had passed through it. Smashed consoles spat sparks of electricity. The floor was carpeted with shards of glass, plastic, and shell casings. Smoke hung in the air, which stank of cordite, blood, and something else that Cordero couldn't identify.

"Smells like gator shit in here," Richards rumbled.

"I don't even want to know how you know that." Cordero stepped through the room, moving around the bulky central terminal where Black had been working.

"Shit!"

He started, finger moving to the trigger. A huge dinosaur lay on the floor before him, bloody jaws open wide, showing rows of gleaming ivory fangs.

He stumbled back, into Richards. "Woah, Chief! What is it?" His eyes bulged when he saw the creature.

Cordero realized that the dinosaur was dead. It lay still, bleeding holes riddled its giant skull and neck.

"There's another one here," Richards said.

Cordero looked around. Another of the creatures lay dead in the shadows beyond the terminal. They were similar in build to the tyrannosaurus that he'd faced earlier, but were smaller, with bony protrusions above their eyes.

He walked along its length, taking in the size of the thing. Whoever had shot it had been careful with their aim. The bullet wounds were clustered around the head and neck. One of its eyes was missing, leaving a bloody gouge where the socket had been.

He stepped around the terminal. There, he found Black.

The technician was still sat where they'd left him, his AR clutched in a death grip. His head hung backwards at an unnatural angle, his skin ghost pale. His fatigues were soaked with blood that leaked from twin lines of puncture wounds along his chest.

"Bite marks," Richards said from over his shoulder. The big man sounded awestruck. "Looks like one of them picked him up and shook him."

Cordero nodded. He approached Black's corpse and removed the dog tags from around his neck. The technician's eyes stared blankly at the ceiling. Cordero gently closed them.

"He got them though."

"Yeah, he did. Hell of a way to go. Taking down two of these monsters by yourself." Richards shook his head. "Never would have thought the little geek had it in him."

Cordero sent Richards to fetch Ortega and Shea. Alone, he leafed through various documents on the desks. Something caught his eye; a portable tablet displaying a wire-frame schematic of the *Buckland;* a red dot blinked on the hull outside a water store. It was the map that Black had mentioned.

"Good job, soldier," he whispered.

"What happened - oh." Cordero looked around. Shea stood by the dead dinosaur, one hand covering her mouth. She stared past Cordero, at Black's body.

"One of your men?" she asked, not taking her eyes off Black.

"A good one." Cordero raised the tablet. "He found the Miyamoto shuttle before these things got to him."

"Let me see." Shea took the tablet from Cordero. She frowned, tapping the screen, making little humming noises as she investigated. Eventually, she looked up.

"I think he's right. There's a power and a data conduit that cross here. It would be the ideal place for them to recharge their batteries and do some data extraction at the same time."

"What's between here and there?"

"Not much. There's a storage hub and one of the water treatment facilities. Nothing too interesting."

"What about dinosaurs? Can you see about those?"

"Not from this," Shea said, raising the tablet. She moved past Cordero to the terminal. "But from here, maybe."

Cordero waited while Shea accessed the computer. He looked around; the devastation around them was extensive. It must have been one hell of a fight.

He had to admit, he'd never expected the technician to go out in such a dramatic fashion.

"There's a lot of damage," Shea interrupted his thoughts. "And things are getting worse. The labs seem stable though. The scanners are showing life forms all over the station, in unusual places too. I would guess that more dinosaurs have come through the portal and gotten loose."

"Black said that the doors had unlocked."

"And opened, too, it appears." She paused. "Some of these life signs could be people."

"Don't get your hopes up," Cordero said, picking up the tablet and Black's AR. It was empty. He put it down across Black's lap. "The station's in a degrading orbit. We need to get to that shuttle."

"Sure, just-" Shea was still staring at the screen. Then, she jumped back. "Woah! What was-"

Cordero came alert. He moved to her side. "What is it?"

"Nothing." She turned and smiled up at him. "It's nothing, don't worry. Just a strange reading on the scanners."

"A dinosaur?"

"No, no. It looked like a power surge. But the readings were odd." She started for the door. "Anyway, never mind. We need to go, right?"

Cordero shook his head. With one final glance at Black, he turned and left the control deck.

SEVENTEEN

The arterial corridor was swamped in darkness.

Cordero took the lead, using the tablet to guide their way. Richards followed close behind, suspiciously eyeing the deep shadows around them. Ortega and Shea were at the rear, the scientist supporting the limping soldier.

Twice, they had to leave the corridor to find alternate routes. Once to avoid a burning cargo truck that was blocking their path; the other when Richards heard growling from up ahead, and Cordero decided not to risk running into something with teeth.

The *Buckland* was dying. Everywhere they went, power was flickering on and off. The air began to taste thick and stale as the fumes from electrical fires overwhelmed the purifiers. Distant alarms shrieked from every direction. Time was short.

None of them mentioned it, though. They all realized the situation they were in. Instead, they focused on moving as fast as they could.

Shortly after emerging back into the arterial for the second time, Cordero spotted a sign for the storage hub. They were on the right track.

He turned to tell the others, and he found that he was floating in midair.

His stomach roiled. The others were floating too. Richards, who had been mid-step, spiraled upwards and bumped his head against the ceiling.

"What's happening?" Richards snarled, pushing off from the ceiling and drifting to the floor.

"The artificial gravity has failed." Shea held tight to Ortega, whose eyes were closed; he didn't seem to notice the change at all. "It could be just in this module, or it could be across the entire station."

Richards spat. The globule of phlegm arrowed away from him to splatter against the wall just behind Cordero. "Well, ain't this a turn up for the books? How're we supposed to get to the shuttle now, swim?"

"Our oxygen tanks." Ortega's voice was a rasping whisper. "They're SOP," he said, grinning at Cordero.

"What about 'em?"

Of course. Cordero tapped the reserve tank on his belt. "It's compressed air. We don't need them to breathe, so we can use them as jets. Let a little air out and off we go. Watch."

He unhooked the canister and aimed it back the way they had come. He tapped the emergency release button gently.

The canister hissed. Cordero was pushed backwards through the air, down the corridor. "See?"

"Oh, I get it." Richards grinned, revealing large, stained teeth. "Like a rocket."

"Exactly." Cordero gestured for the others to follow. "We just need a little bit of thrust."

Richards got the idea quickly enough. Shea did too, but she didn't have a canister of her own so had to use Ortega's, who clung on to her weakly. On her first attempt, she pressed the button too hard, and they crashed into a wall. Ortega gave a yelp of pain.

"Here, I got him," Richards said, carefully taking Ortega's limp form from Shea. He tore a strip of fabric from his combat webbing and used it to carefully tie Ortega to his chest. "You keep yourself safe, ok?"

Shea nodded. "Thanks," she said, but Richards had already turned away.

Through careful use of their tanks, they managed to make good time. It wasn't long before Cordero spotted the entrance to the storage hub.

"Hold up," he warned the others, grabbing the door frame to stop his forward momentum.

The storage hub was larger even than the Nexus Chamber. It was three stories high, as tall as the station itself, with huge cargo doors on each floor. Shipping containers, each the size of a truck, crashed together in the wide-open space. One wall was entirely made up of thick plexiglass. Jagged cracks spidered crazily along its length.

A hand slapped down on his shoulder.

"This it?" Richards stared around the storage hub. "Something made a mess of this place."

"Once the gravity went, all it would have taken was one slight movement to turn the entire thing into a zero-g bowling alley," Shea said, floating just over his right shoulder.

"We got to cross through *that?*" Richards asked, staring in horror at the asteroid field of steel boxes.

Cordero nodded, checking the tablet. He pointed. "We need to get up there."

Richards and Shea followed his finger. Directly opposite where they stood, two floors up, a set of doors juddered open and closed.

"Great," Richards said. "Just great. We're gonna get smashed flat the second we go out there."

"The stairs have been destroyed, too," Shea said. Her voice was calm, but she was tapping her fingers nervously against her thigh. A crushed, twisted mess of metal spun slowly in the center of the room, attached to the floor by a frayed cable.

"We need to find another way round, man," Richards said, looking back the way they had come.

The station chose that moment to judder violently. A warning siren began to sound close by.

"We don't have time. This is the fastest way."

"But it's suicide to go out there." Richards shook his head, hands bunched into fists.

Ortega, who up until now Cordero had thought was unconscious, lifted his head. "Just go, man. We stay, we die for sure."

"But..." Richards's mouth hung open, eyes darting left and right as he searched for the right words. "Fine," he said resignedly. "Fine. Me and you go first, ok?"

Ortega smiled thinly. "I'm ready if you are."

Richard rolled his eyes. "I'm always ready."

He knelt, careful to avoid bumping Ortega, then straightened his legs suddenly, flinging them into the storage bay. His aim was good; from where Cordero was standing, they were headed right towards the second-floor exit.

Spinning shipping containers soared around Richards and Ortega as they flew through the air. Cordero, rapt, winced in horrified anticipation as a partially shredded container brushed close enough to hit the SAW strapped to Richards's back with a hollow clang.

The pair were halfway across the room when something enormous flew from within the maelstrom of containers.

It was a dinosaur the size of a bus. A pair of thick horns protruded from its frilled skull and another above a sharp beak. It sailed through the air, bellowing, heading straight for Richards and Ortega, its four stumpy legs thrashing in frustration.

Cordero and Shea could only watch in horror.

"How the hell did a triceratops get in here?" Shea murmured.

Richards tried to twist in the air to face the new threat, reaching for the gun in his back. But even as he turned, the triceratops was upon them.

It missed them by a few feet, sailing past and smashing into a container, which burst apart in a spray of frozen cafeteria food. The triceratops was barely slowed down, crashing through another pair of containers before hitting the far wall. In its confusion, it then pushed back into the open void, spitting blood.

Richards and Ortega, by this point, had reached the far side of the room. Richards snagged hold of a railing and pulled them down to safety inside of the doorway.

The triceratops continued to bounce around in a maddened rage. It glanced off a ceiling beam and slammed into the viewing window like a battering ram. The crack in the window, Cordero noticed, seemed wider.

They didn't have long. "You should go next," he said to Shea.

She shook her head, fear flashing in her eyes. "I… I don't think I can," she said. "Not on my own."

"No problem. We can go together."

He extended a hand. She took it. Her hand felt small and soft in his. He crouched, getting ready to leap, and he saw her imitating him out of the corner of his eye. He could feel her pulse racing through her hand.

Cordero took a steadying breath. "No matter what happens, keep your focus on the doorway." He gave her a smile. She returned it, although he could feel the falseness of it. He understood that.

"And remember," he said, "I'll be here. No matter what. I'm right here."

She smiled again. It seemed more real this time.

There was no point in waiting any longer. He leapt.

Things went wrong almost immediately. The triceratops crashed into a container and ricocheted off, on an intercept route with Cordero and Shea. Its head was tucked down, the two sharp horns aimed directly at them.

Distracted by the sight, neither of them noticed the jagged remains of a shipping container coming towards them until the last minute. Cordero shouted in surprise. Startled, Shea let go of his hand.

Moving quickly, Cordero grasped Shea around the waist and flung her towards Richards. She yelled in frustration as she flew away from Cordero, the distance between them growing as he drifted backwards from the counter-momentum.

Cordero grimaced at the furious look on her face before the triceratops barreled between them, blocking his view.

Cordero hit the floor. Without slowing, he pushed off, aiming at a container close by. He bumped gently against the side and pressed himself flat. He glanced up; Richards was helping Shea back to the ground. She'd made it, at least.

The triceratops roared past his container, towards the viewing window. Cordero clung on and waited. The container rotated lazily, until eventually he was facing the others.

He couldn't afford to wait. The dinosaur could come crashing back at any moment. It was trapped, miserably ricocheting from wall to wall; every pass it made was another chance for him to get crushed to atoms.

Another container drifted close by. Cordero waited until it got close enough, then he jumped.

He tensed, out in the open, waiting for the triceratops to come bellowing towards him. Then, he found himself in darkness, inside the hollowed container.

Other containers floated between Cordero and his team. This looked to be the way to safety; short hops between containers, hopefully avoiding the triceratops.

He crawled along the container's interior to the look out. The triceratops was falling blindly towards the closest wall, trailing blood, and shit. If he timed this right, he would cross to another container before it got anywhere close.

Three. Two. One.

Cordero bounced up, into the open. No sooner had he done so than he heard an ear-splitting roar.

The triceratops had seen him. It was furious in its madness. It lunged off the wall towards him, horns down.

Cordero crashed onto a container and lost sight of the approaching triceratops. He scrabbled around, trying to find it again.

Then, everything exploded.

Everything went black. Cordero felt himself spinning through the air, spikes of pain jabbing all over his body.

He opened his eyes. The room spun around him, a cloud of shredded metal and torn fabric accompanying him in his flight.

The triceratops must have hit the container he was on and knocked him loose in the room. He grasped for the oxygen canister, hoping to stop himself spinning at least, but it was gone from his harness.

He tried to work out which direction he was heading, the effort making him nauseous.

He was spinning straight towards the crack in the center of the viewing window.

Cordero braced for the impact. He tried to let his muscles relax, so as not to tense up too much. This was going to hurt.

He stopped with a jolt.

Someone was holding him by the shoulders. He heard a grunt as whoever was holding him braced against his weight.

"Hey, Mike."

Cordero looked up. Ortega was looking down at him. He was stood upright on the window, arms extended over his head, the blackness of space between his feet. He gripped Cordero by the shoulders.

"What're you doing here, Juan?"

"I jumped down to help you out, buddy."

"Why?"

"I still owe you for Colombia, Mike." Ortega pulled Cordero down towards him. Cordero tucked in his knees, rotating himself in mid-air, until his feet touched the glass and he was face-to face with Ortega.

The surface beneath his feet wasn't even, he realized. Looking down, he saw that they were stood on top of the crack in the window. It looked larger than it had before.

Ortega looked awful. His skin had lost its color, he was almost white. Black shadows gathered beneath bloodshot eyes. He grinned, thin lips parting to show starkly white teeth. One of his hands had gone to his abdomen, where thick blood oozed through the bandages wrapped around his stomach.

"You shouldn't have come back for me."

Ortega shrugged. "I saw how you were flailing around out there. Like a turd flushed down the pan. You weren't getting back yourself."

Cordero wanted to tell Ortega that he should go back, that he should leave him behind. But there was no time. The triceratops was falling towards them.

"We have to go. Now."

"You don't need to tell me twice," Ortega croaked. He jumped.

Ortega's sudden departure surprised Cordero. It took him a few seconds to gather himself before he jumped after his friend. He angled towards the exit, where Richards was gripping the railing, his mouth moving soundlessly.

He had barely gone more than a few meters when he realized his mistake.

The triceratops hadn't been heading straight towards them, it had been moving at an angle; and now it was on a direct interception course with him.

Cordero looked around frantically, hoping to warn Ortega, but he was nowhere to be seen.

"Juan?"

There. Ortega was to his left, crouched on a wall. He was already out of danger.

As Cordero watched, trapped on a collision course with the beast, Ortega pushed off from the wall.

He was heading straight for the triceratops.

"No!" Cordero realized, too late, what Ortega was attempting. "Juan, stop!"

But it was too late.

The triceratops got closer. It seemed to fill the world, a roaring freight train bearing down upon him.

Ortega came in from the left and landed on the beast's back, just behind its neck frill. He bounced off at first, but grasped the bony horn and clung on.

The triceratops bucked and bellowed, swinging its head from side to side. But Ortega held on with a death grip, blood leaking from his bandage forming a red cloud around him.

When Cordero was a few dozen feet from the triceratops, Ortega raised his oxygen canister over his head, aiming it up and away from Cordero. He pressed and held his thumb down on the emergency release.

Compressed air burst from the canister. The sudden explosion of gas slammed Ortega down against the triceratops's body. His chin caught the edge of its neck frill and blood sprayed from his jaw. But he still held on.

The blast of air was enough to move the triceratops's mass. It was jolted to one side, at an angle away from Cordero, accelerating rapidly.

It passed Cordero by inches. He locked eyes with Ortega as he passed. Ortega was smiling through a mask of blood.

Then he was gone, heading directly towards the crack in the window.

Ortega tried to leap clear. But he was too slow and had lost too much blood.

Cordero hit a wall hard. The wall grunted and gave way. Strong arms wrapped around him and he heard Richards's voice in his ear.

"Got you, Chief. I got you."

They were in a corridor, the storage bay visible through the doorway they must have passed through. Richards was pressed against the wall, holding tight to Cordero.

Cordero shook himself free and pushed past Shea into the storage hub. She shouted after him, but he didn't stop.

"Juan!"

He grasped the railing and looked down into the room, just in time to see the triceratops smash into the window. Directly into the center, where the crack was widest.

The window exploded with a percussive boom.

Shea shouted something, but it was lost in the roaring of air as the storage bay decompressed rapidly.

The triceratops was dragged screeching through the breach, the sharp edges tearing the flesh from its bones. Ortega still clung to its back.

"Juan!"

Ortega looked up.

And then he was gone, leaving behind a thick welter of blood.

Cordero stared blankly at the space where his friend had been. Even as the pressure sucked the air from his lungs and his skin from his bones, he couldn't move. Couldn't think. Could do nothing but stare.

"You didn't owe me for anything," he said soundlessly.

And then he was yanked backwards through the bulkhead doors, which slammed shut firmly.

Cordero lay on the floor. Through the fuzz of his thoughts, he gradually realized that gravity was back, and there was air flowing back into his lungs.

But his friend, his only friend, was gone.

EIGHTEEN

"Are you ok?"

Cordero sat up. Shea knelt beside him, concern on her face.

He nodded mutely. Right then, he couldn't trust himself to speak, afraid of what might come tumbling out.

Shea seemed to understand. She smiled softly at Cordero and reached out a hand. He took it and pulled himself up.

"Thanks," he said, dusting himself off. His hand came away smeared red. He looked down. There was blood all over his fatigues. He patted himself down to find the source of bleeding.

It was Ortega's blood.

He almost sat right back down again; the tiredness came upon him so suddenly. Every one of his muscles seemed to lose all energy and become like jelly. His stomach roiled and he tasted acid in the back of his throat.

It was Richards that brought him back to reality.

"Those motherfucking dinosaurs!" the big man screamed, storming from one side of the corridor to the other. "They killed two of ours. This is too much, man!"

"Three," Cordero said wearily. "They got MacTiernan."

"Oh that's just great, that's just what I needed to hear." Richards threw the SAW to the floor in disgust. It clattered into the far corner. "There's no way we're getting off this fucking station alive. I tell you, this place is cursed. Everyone who's been here has died. And we're next."

"I stayed alive," she whispered. Richards turned his furious gaze upon her, making her wince.

"I've been wondering about that. I find it mighty suspicious that everyone on this abattoir is dead except for you, a puny little geek. And a woman, too." He spat.

"You better can that shit, Richards," Cordero said. "You need to get a grip."

Richards bristled, pulling himself up to his full height. "And who are you to tell me what to do?"

"You know who I am. I'm the guy who kept you alive in worse places than this."

"There are no worse places than this." Richards hammered a massive fist into the wall, leaving behind a bloody smear from his torn knuckles. "Nobody has been in a place like this before."

"Remember Tuscany station, when something got into the water supply and turned everybody crazy?"

Richards stared at the wall, arms loose at his side. "Yeah, I remember."

"There must've been five hundred blood-crazy bastards running around on that station. And every one of them wanted to cut us open and eat our guts. Did we die then?"

Richard shook his head.

"Did we give up?"

"No."

"What about the Typhoon Larosa? Those terrorists were ready to kill themselves if it took us with them. And did they?"

Richards turned to face Cordero. He was still breathing heavily, and his hands were clenched into tight fists, but he was calmer than before.

"All right, I take your point."

"Good man. Now come on, we have a shuttle waiting."

Richards picked the SAW up off the ground and followed Cordero, who was studying the tablet as he walked, sparing a single glance back towards the unremarkable bulkhead doors that marked the final resting place of his oldest friend.

He wanted to say something to mark the occasion. But no words came. No words, no nothing. I don't even have his dog tags, Cordero thought. Not that there was anyone to return them to; Ortega hadn't had any family to speak of, no one who would miss him.

No one except Cordero.

Shea caught up with him. They walked in companionable silence for a while, watching Richards, who had started to range ahead, jabbing the SAW into every dark corner.

"How are you?" she asked eventually.

"Surviving," Cordero said. They walked on without speaking for a while, the ceiling lights getting dimmer the further they went. Cordero could feel her concern. But didn't want to talk. He just wanted to get them off this doomed orbital.

"You shouldn't care so much," he said eventually, when her glances became too much.

"What do you mean?"

"About us. We're your ticket off this place. We came here to retrieve what we could. That's you. You don't need to worry about us, we're just doing our jobs."

Shea didn't reply. He looked at her. Her eyebrows were raised, her brow furrowed.

"Of course I care. You're hurting. I know how that is. I've lost a lot of colleagues - a lot of *friends* today." She paused. The silence lengthened. "I don't like to see others hurting."

"No." He stared into the gloom. "Neither do I."

Shea glanced at him. "You made an interesting career choice for a man who doesn't like to see others in pain."

He nodded, feeling numb. "Don't I know it."

They walked on, through the darkness that shrouded them like a suffocating blanket, using the light of the tablet's screen to guide their way. The device had just begun to bleep a low battery warning when Richards called back.

"Water storage facility up ahead. We're here."

By the time Cordero and Shea caught up, Richards had already climbed the short set of stairs into the water store. Cordero felt a flash of frustration at his lack of caution, but quickly suppressed it. They weren't a ROR team anymore. They were exhausted survivors. Throwing reprimands around would do no good now.

Instead, he led Shea up the stairs. They emerged into a room cast in a pale blue light. Richards greeted them gruffly.

"What took you lovebirds so long?" Richards chuckled.

Shea scowled but Cordero just laughed. He waved the tablet. "This is the place, according to Black's calculations."

He looked around. He'd hoped there would be some obvious sign of the Miyamoto team's infiltration: a hastily sealed hole in the hull, or an exterior hatch.

But there was nothing. The room, though large, was almost completely bare. A bulky generator rumbled away in one corner, turning a pair of fans atop an enormous water tank, a cylinder two stories tall and so wide it took up most of the room. There were viewing portholes spaced evenly around the cylinder; the blue light leaking out through them was the sole source of illumination in the room. An emergency hull breach locker stood against the wall, a mandatory fixture in any area of the station that adjoined the void of space. Almost hidden in the shadows cast by the generator and the water tank was a small closet door, the only other exit from the room.

Cordero stepped up to one of the portholes and pressed his face to the glass.

A set of razor-sharp teeth lunged towards him.

Cordero fell back onto the ground, his hands grasping for a weapon that was no longer there.

Richards ran over. "What happened?"

"There's something in there." Cordero waved his hand at the tank.

"*In* there?" Shea stepped up to look.

"Careful," Cordero muttered, embarrassed at being taken by surprise.

Shea looked back at him. "Don't worry. This is three-inch plastiglass. It'd take an explosion to breach it." She stood on her tip toes and peered into the tank. "Woah."

Richards helped Cordero back to his feet. Together, they joined Shea at the porthole.

At first, Cordero could only see the soft blue water. Then, he saw something moving. It seemed to drift with the current, like a strand of Sargasso. But there was no current in the tank.

It was a neck, Cordero released. A long serpentine neck topped by a triangular head. Cordero followed the neck down to a broad yet sleek body with paddle-like flippers that twisted slowly in the water.

"It's a plesiosaur," Shea said. She turned to look at the others. "How the hell did it get in there?"

Richards shrugged. "It's some kind of water dinosaur. Makes sense to me that it's in the water."

"How'd it get in there, though?"

"Through the Nexus Portal." Richards furrowed his brow. "Right?"

"And the triceratops in the storage bay?" Shea seemed lost in thought. "Those doors weren't big enough for it to get through. I knew there was something off about those energy readings..."

"We need to keep on track here," Cordero interrupted. He gestured to the tablet. "We're on the clock, remember?"

"Right, right." Shea seemed to mentally shake herself. "What's the plan?"

"Spread out," he said. "Check for anything unusual. If Black was right, Schaefer's team came aboard somewhere around here."

"And if Black was wrong?" Shea asked.

Cordero grimaced. "Let's handle one problem at a time."

They spread out to search the room. Richards went over to the generator, giving the water tank a wide berth. Shea lingered near the entrance.

Cordero paced along the curved exterior wall. It followed the curvature of the modular station. The wall was made up of prefabricated panels, molded to fit neatly between rib-like girders. There was a narrow crawl space behind the wall, Cordero knew, and then another paneled wall. Beyond that lay the cold of space.

The *Buckland* was essentially no different to the hundreds like it that Lulworth had in orbit around Earth, all made to a standard modular design. The company was a late arrival in the race into space. Unlike other mega-corporations, who had rushed to launch cheap orbitals to quickly exploit the lack of legislation off-Earth, Lulworth had invested heavily into developing a single factory station. It had cost them almost a decade and billions of e-dollars, but it had proven to be the company's making. Now, while other mega-corps had to shuttle pieces of their stations to space and painstakingly assemble them in orbit, Lulworth was able to churn out a dozen every year.

Cordero reached the end of the wall. He had seen nothing unusual. He sucked his teeth; he must have missed something.

He turned around and headed back, more slowly this time.

He almost missed it. Next to the emergency locker, one of the panels stuck out more than the others. At first glance, it could easily be taken for a manufacturing error.

He peered at the panel and felt a surge of certainty. At the spot where the panel joined the girder, the telltale smudging of recent welding could be seen.

"Hey!" he shouted. Shea looked up from where she stood against the far wall. He couldn't see Richards. "I think I've found it."

"We got a problem, Chief." Richards's voice came from the closet doorway. "There's a fuel store back here."

Richards stood in an open doorway. Behind him, flames filled the closet.

NINETEEN

"How the hell did that start?"

"No idea." Richards lumbered over, closing the door behind him. Cordero could still hear the flames crackling. "But it's been burning for a while. And we don't have long till those fuel canisters blow."

Cordero indicated the loose panel. "Here's where they came on board. This panel's been removed. I need you to help me remove it."

Richards looked skeptical. "That's solid steel. We can't just pull it loose."

"Which is why they make us carry these." Cordero unhooked the portable welding tool from his harness. "SOP."

"Company regulations finally make sense." Richards rolled his eyes, but he grinned at the same time. He braced against the panel. "Go to town, Chief."

Cordero lit the welding torch. The flame was blinding in the softly lit room. Squinting, he applied the flame to the edge of the panel. It burned brightly red and liquid metal ran down to the floor.

The steel gave easily beneath the bright hot flame, further evidence of recent tampering. The smell of burning metal was strong in his nostrils. Or was it the fire in the fuel store? He began to move quicker.

"Careful, Chief. Don't burn your fingers off."

"Nearly there," Cordero said through gritted teeth. "Got it."

The panel came loose suddenly. Richards grunted, taking its full weight on his shoulders. With Cordero's help, they lowered it to the floor.

"Here." Shea had three emergency space suits in her arms. "I found these in the locker. There's oxygen masks and tanks too."

They quickly suited up. The suits hung loosely on Shea and Cordero, being one-size-fits-all. Richards's broad frame came close to splitting his suit's shoulders. They took it in turns to check the fastenings of the full-enclosure masks and the connections on their oxygen tanks. Cordero inhaled deeply, enjoying the clean, sterile air. It made him realize just how strong the smell of smoke had been.

Richards went to pick up the SAW, but Cordero shook his head. "Too bulky," he said, though his voice was muffled by the mask.

Richards dropped the gun. They squeezed through the opening into the crawl space. It was a tight fit, and there was no flooring; they stood on support beams, beneath which the wall curved away into darkness.

Cordero found one of the safety hooks situated through the crawl space, used by maintenance staff to keep themselves safe, and clipped the safety line from his harness onto it. The safety line was an extendable cable made from high-tensile wire. It was strong enough to lift a tank. The others found hooks of their own.

Satisfied that everyone was secure, Cordero climbed sideways along the beams, following the curve of the wall. He felt that he could feel the void of space, inches away through the skin of steel.

It didn't take long for him to find where the Miyamoto team had cut into the outer layer of the *Buckland's* exterior wall. A Dolman patch - a vacuum packed piece of nano plastic that expanded to fill tears in the hulls of starships and space stations - covered a hastily carved hole, roughly man-sized. Dolman patches were designed for quick fixes, and for quick removals.

Cordero located the release bump on the surface of the patch. He looked back at the other two, double checking that they were fixed to the security hook. Richards gave him a brusque nod; Shea raised a hand nervously.

Cordero pressed down on the bump. The pressure caused a reaction in the patch's nanobots. Activated, they began to devour the solid plastic.

Almost immediately, the patch crumbled away. Air rushed out of the hole. Cordero was jolted forwards. He felt the ragged edge of the tear pull at his suit, hard. For a horrible moment he thought that it was breached, and he tensed, bracing himself for the decompression.

He opened his eyes. He was floating in open space.

He hung a few meters away from the *Buckland's* hull. The safety line extended from his harness back through the hole in the station's surface. Like an umbilical cord, he thought crazily. Shea and Richards floated nearby, surrounded by a cloud of detritus from the water storage room.

He took a moment to scan the station's surface. It was plain and utilitarian, a design aesthetic common for Lulworth facilities. The only features breaking up the smooth, grey hull were radar dishes and sensor bulbs scattered haphazardly across the surface.

Except for one bulb. Larger than the rest, it clung to the station like a cancerous growth. Cordero knew that it wasn't part of the station's sensor array. It was too large.

Large enough to house a team of commandos. It had to be the Miyamoto shuttle.

Using the safety cable, Cordero dragged himself back to the *Buckland.* Reaching the hull, he found another safety hook, tucked beside a radar dish. He grabbed it for support, then pressed the line's fast release on his harness. Inside the station, Cordero's cable unclipped itself from the safety hook and retracted rapidly, slowing for the last few meters to tuck neatly away into his suit's harness.

Arm over arm, Cordero pulled himself towards the shuttle. Richards and Shea, following his lead, retracted their lines then secured themselves to the exterior. Shea found another safety hook, while Richards settled for the thick neck of a radar dish.

As Cordero got closer, the shuttle's camouflage became less effective. Up close, it stood out starkly. It was a thing of sleek curves and careful construction. No join lines on its surface betrayed the assembly process, aside from a thin line along the nose that he presumed was the entrance. Subtle bulges on the lower side began to look like engine exhausts.

They made good time. Cordero took the lead with Shea following close behind. Richards brought up the rear. The big man was not a natural climber, least of all in zero gravity.

They were just over halfway to the shuttle when the station seemed to swell.

Cordero didn't hear the explosion. But he felt it in the violent shaking of the hull.

His comm unit crackled to life. "Have we already re-entered the atmosphere?" Richards's deep baritone was tinged with panic.

The hull exploded outwards.

The entire side of the station, where they had been climbing moments before, peeled open. Tongues of flame burst out, sending scything shards of steel exploding outwards in a razor cloud.

The water from the tank followed. Gallons and gallons of water sprayed into space, instantly freezing as it exited the station.

Cordero held on tightly to the *Buckland*, barely able to cling on. Pain coursed through his fingertips as the station fought to shake him loose.

Something huge burst from the tear in the station hull.

The plesiosaur was thrown forcefully from the *Buckland,* trapped in a rapidly freezing ball of water. Its long neck thrashed back and forth, jaws opening and closing in a silent screech as its eyeballs were pulled from its skull.

Cordero watched, frozen in horror, as the creature's head lashed down towards Richards. Richards threw up his arms to cover his face as the plesiosaur's jaws clamped across his chest, spraying bone and frozen blood.

The plesiosaur twisted, ripping Richards's ribs open, exposing his lungs. Gore fountained from his mouth, the thrashing of the plesiosaur spraying it in a wide arc.

Richards, near death, clung grimly to the hull. Its jaws anchored in Richards's body; the plesiosaur's body whipped over Cordero's head. Just as it reached the extent of its swing, Richards's grip finally gave. The monster and the man came loose from the *Buckland,* smashing right into the shuttle, which tore loose, the landing grips sunk deeply into the station's skin no match for the impact of the prehistoric terror.

Cordero could only watch in stunned horror as the plesiosaur, his comrade and the shuttle spun off into space, taking their only escape route with them.

TWENTY

"Cordero, can you hear me?"

The voice came from somewhere inside his oxygen mask. It was tinny and riddled with static but was unmistakably Shea.

She clung to the shattered stem of a radar dish, drifting like a leaf in the wind in the aftermath of the explosion. Something long and thin dangled from her waist; it was her safety wire, severed through the middle.

He quickly clambered over to her and pulled her back to the station surface. Removing his wire from the safety hook, he attached the other end to her.

She arched an eyebrow at him. "So, if one of us falls, we both die?"

"I won't let you die," he said.

She stared back at him. "I believe you," she said after a moment.

Neither of them spoke. Cordero took in the devastation around them.

The station was venting oxygen; crystallizing gouts of gas coughed from the tear in the hull. He though back to their journey across the *Buckland*. Without the life support systems working, they had to assume that most of the station was now airless and cold.

He checked the gauge on his oxygen tank. Less than half an hour left. Emergency tanks weren't designed for prolonged use, instead they were intended to provide just enough air to escape breached sections of orbital stations.

"How much air do you have left, Shea?" he asked.

Shea checked her own gauge. "Maybe twenty minutes." Her voice was calm, but he could see the fear in her eyes.

"Probably not enough to get back inside and find somewhere with active life support."

It wasn't a question, but she answered it anyway. "A hull breach like this will have hopelessly compromised the *Buckland*. It's not built to take much in the way of punishment."

"The company doesn't like to spend money if they can help it," Cordero said bitterly. "If they churn orbitals out cheaply enough, they can afford to lose a few each year."

"You'd think the human cost would be factored in, somehow." There was venom in Shea's tone.

Cordero laughed. "You know as well as I do there's no liability costs out here. Once you agree to work in orbit, you've agreed to travel outside the law. And corps don't make a habit of paying anything for dead staff."

"I was talking about the cost in lives."

Cordero shrugged. "As far as the company's concerned, life is cheap."

Shea let out a sad sigh. She changed the subject. "If there was anywhere on the *Buckland* likely to survive intact after the explosion, it would be the labs."

"Of course." While everything else about the *Buckland* conformed to standard Company orbital schematics, the central laboratory complex had clearly been built for a specific purpose. "Makes sense, Lulworth would want to protect its investment."

"Yeah, well." Shea turned her head to stare out at the blue and green planet spread out before them. The reflection of the Earth on her visor obscured her face. "Even that extra expenditure isn't going to help once this thing enters orbit. How long do we have?"

Cordero shrugged. "The tablet was our only way of monitoring the station's location, and I have no idea where that's gone. Can't be long left now though."

"So, the question is, what's going to kill us first, re-entry or suffocation?"

"At least it's not dinosaurs," Shea said.

"Unless you want to chance going through the Nexus Portal," he grinned.

They both laughed hollowly. "Let's stick with just the two ways to die," Cordero said bleakly.

"Two ways is more than enough-" Shea went silent. Cordero turned to look at her. She had an intense look on her face, her brow furrowed. She was chewing on her lip intently.

He put a hand on her shoulder. "Are you ok?"

"Two ways..."

Shea suddenly turned to Cordero. Her eyes shone and a broad smile lit up her face.

"Two ways, Cordero! A door goes two ways!"

Cordero just stared. "And?"

Shea huffed, rolling her eyes at his inability to keep up with her thought process.

"We can take advantage of the principle of transference, of the effect created when objects pass through the portal. If we can get back to the Nexus, I'll be able to make a few adjustments to the program. It'll just take me a little time, taking into account the likely variables in quantum oscillation..."

She tailed off into distracted mumbling. Cordero snapped his fingers. There was no sound in the vacuum, of course. He clapped himself on the head.

"Shea," he said. She stopped her flow of technobabble and focused her gaze on him.

"Sorry," she said. "The details might be a little over your head."

"Can you give me the broad strokes?" He held up a hand as she took in a breath. "*Without* making it too much of a science lesson."

She laughed breathily. "Did you even graduate high school? Never mind," she chuckled as he began to object. "It didn't occur to me until a moment ago; a doorway goes two ways. The Nexus Portal is open to our time, here on the station. On the other side, it's open to North America, in the Cretaceous. But I think I can change where the portal is open to one side without closing the door to the other side."

Cordero blinked. "How... that, that doesn't make any sense."

"But I think it will work," Shea said. "My theory partly explains the plesiosaur in the water tank. And probably the triceratops in the storage room, too."

"How?"

"The transference principles. A problem we had with the Nexus Project was getting the portals to remain where we aimed them. Sometimes, our test subjects appeared somewhere other than where they should have. That's what those strange energy readings I saw in the control deck looked like; the portal misfiring and popping out the dinosaurs across the station."

"So how does that help us now?"

"That same principle of transference, that changes the spatial targeting, can also affect the temporal. We can reprogram the door so that when we go through into the Cretaceous, when we return, we return into another time."

"So, we go through into the past, then come back into the present?"

Shea nodded vigorously. "Uh huh. Though it's just a theory that's never been tested before. We could end up stuck in the past, or torn apart by the energies of the transference."

"Alright." He flexed his shoulders. "It's risky, but it's what we've got. We've got twenty minutes to get to the   lab.   Let's   move."

TWENTY-ONE

"Is this the place?"

Cordero and Shea hung onto the side of the *Buckland.* They were midway down one of the spokes that joined the arterial exterior ring of the station with the labs complex in the center.

"I'm fairly sure." Shea sounded hesitant.

"Fairly sure?" He couldn't keep the skepticism out of his voice.

"It's the best I can do. I can't remember the entire floor plan."

"Then let's go with what we have." He was breathing shallowly, trying to conserve the oxygen in the tank. They had swapped tanks before they'd set off. Shea hadn't wanted the fuller tank, but he had insisted. The quickest way to reach the labs was over the top of the *Buckland's* hull. It had been a slow, exhausting climb, and she had needed the extra.

Cordero checked his tank. Five minutes remaining. Time to get cutting.

It took only a few short cuts with the welding torch to tear open the station hull. Cordero squeezed through into the crawl space. The station's artificial gravity took a sudden firm hold, and his body became heavier. Shea followed, stumbling as she entered the artificial gravity field.

"You got the seal?" he asked.

Shea nodded, pulling the Dolman patch from a pouch in her space suit. She tore the wrapping; the patch activated and expanded quickly to fill the tear.

Once the breach was sealed, Cordero used the remaining fuel in the torch to cut through the inside wall. Together, they stepped through into an airless corridor.

They headed towards the hub. After a short walk, they reached an airlock. Shea cycled it open and they entered the next chamber. The airlock continued its cycle, and after a short wait a light on the wall turned green, indicating that a breathable atmosphere had been restored.

Cordero released the catch on his mask. Blood rushed painfully back into his face as the tight straps came loose.

He took a deep, cleansing breath. "It's good to be back," he said sardonically.

Shea removed her mask and shook her hair loose. "It's good that there's still power here," she said, moving over to a console on the wall. She tapped a key, and the inner door began its opening cycle. "Though the security doors are still open throughout the lab complex."

"So Barney could be anywhere?" Cordero said, as the airlock door finished cycling open. He stepped out of the airlock, into a room that looked like the room they'd found Markovitz's body in. It felt like a thousand years ago, not a handful of hours. The room was virtually bare, aside from a smattering of broken lab equipment. He picked up a length of iron bar from amongst the shattered remains of a desk.

Shea joined him, looking around the room with interest. "Barney?"

"The tyrannosaurus."

"Oh, right. Hopefully it's gone back through the portal."

"Letting something worse come through."

"You're such an optimist," Shea laughed.

"Some would say a realist. I prefer to prepare for the worst."

"And hope for the best?" Shea asked.

"I don't waste my time doing that."

Shea wasn't listening. She made a beeline for the Nexus Chamber. She didn't even wait for him, she just barreled on through.

Cordero winced and hustled after her. She would need someone to watch her back.

Nothing had changed since he had last been here. The portal was still open, a rippling blur in the air inside the arch of the Nexus machine.

Shea was already stood at one of the consoles, tapping in command after command, her fingers a blur over the keys.

"Need any help?" he asked, but Shea didn't respond, too focused on her work.

Time to make myself useful, Cordero thought. If his guess were correct, they had entered the Nexus room on the opposite side from the airlock he'd come through before. The airlock opposite was still open. On the wall, he again clocked the sign for the Purification Chamber and Cryogenics.

He headed across the room towards the other airlock, stepping over the ruined bodies of scientists and Miyamoto operatives alike. The dead were beginning to rot. He started to breathe through his mouth. He scanned the floor, hoping to find an abandoned firearm, but there was nothing in sight. It looked like he was stuck with the iron bar.

His foot struck something hard. He glanced down.

It was a shock stick. He'd used them before. Essentially a cattle prod, but designed for use against humans. Corporate police and military forces used them for riot control on Earth. They were non-lethal yet incredibly painful, ideal for putting down workers's rights protests that got out of control.

Cordero wasn't sure how much use it would be against the thick skin of a dinosaur, but it had to be better than a metal bar. He discarded the bar and picked up the shock stick, testing its reassuring weight.

He walked back to Shea. "Why is there a cryogenic chamber on this station?"

"Huh?" Shea looked up, distracted. "Oh, it's for preserving samples. Not useful for this experiment, but we didn't know what would happen when test subjects went through the portal."

The console bleeped alarmingly, and Shea cursed. "Cordero," she said, as she bent over the console. "We're going to need to replace one of the transformers to get this going. Can you check the storeroom while I fix this thing?"

"Sure thing." He headed back towards the airlock, hoping that the tyrannosaurus hadn't gone into the store. It seemed unlikely, not with the room being so dark. It had seemed to struggle with the low light level before.

Still, he stepped carefully as he approached the airlock. A tyrannosaurus was a large animal, one unlikely to remain silent even if it were trying.

The airlock lights were out. Both doors were open. The storeroom beyond swam in inky darkness.

Cordero stepped into the airlock.

A growl came from the storeroom.

"Barney..."

TWENTY-TWO

Beady eyes glimmered, fixed on Cordero. He backed away, raising the shock stick. He thumbed the activation switch; magnetic coils around the stick's head sparked with electricity.

A low growl rumbled from the dark, so low that Cordero could feel it in his chest. Dagger-like teeth gleamed in the light of the shock stick.

"Hello again, you purple fucker," Cordero murmured.

The tyrannosaurus roared.

The sound was overwhelming. Cordero gritted his teeth and squeezed his eyes closed as the stench of rotting meat and thick globules of saliva spattered over him.

He ran back into the Nexus Chamber, heading away from where Shea stood at the console.

"Shea!" he shouted. "Hide!"

She looked up, eyes widening when she saw the tyrannosaurus emerging from the airlock. She didn't think twice, dropping behind the console and curling into a tight ball.

The tyrannosaurus crashed into the Nexus Chamber, roaring. It stepped onto the walkway, which crumpled beneath its weight, sending it stumbling into the center of the room. It crashed to the floor but immediately righted itself, head swiveling to lock onto Cordero.

Cordero pumped his legs and arms like pistons, powering across the chamber. He felt the floor shaking as the tyrannosaurus began to follow him. That was good; he had to keep it away from Shea.

There was another airlock ahead. Cordero ran straight through it. He found himself in another storeroom, largely bare aside from a stack of shipping crates against one wall. There was another door, labelled *Cryogenics,* just beyond them. A warehouse crane loomed in one corner, nearly touching the ceiling, and a forklift suit stood alongside it. Pipes lined the walls. Cordero touched one as he passed; it was hot, probably steam.

Cordero ran up to the forklift. It was a beast of a machine; twelve feet of painted yellow steel, with a pair of powerful robotic arms, ending in pneumatic claws the operator would use to move shipping crates. The driver's cabin was protected by a mesh and steel frame. Cordero climbed onto the mounting step and let out a satisfied grunt; the keys were in the ignition.

If he were going to have to face Barney, he'd rather do so from inside the mech suit.

A roar came from behind him, terrifyingly close.

He spun. The tyrannosaurus was already in the room. It lunged at him, jaws wide.

Cordero dove aside, hitting the ground rolling. Behind him, the tyrannosaurus crashed into the forklift and sent it crashing to the ground. One foot crunched down on the driver's cabin, mangling it beyond repair.

Time for a new plan, Cordero thought, as the tyrannosaurus turned to face him and roared.

The floor beneath him was made up of thick mesh grilles laid over a narrow crawl space.

Without pausing to think twice, he knelt and heaved the closest grille loose. The tyrannosaurus stomped towards him, crossing the distance between them in two strides.

Cordero dropped through the gap.

The tyrannosaurus's jaws snapped shut right above him, missing him by a hair.

Cordero crawled forwards on his belly. The tyrannosaurus followed, its immense weight causing the grilles to bend beneath it.

There was a wall ahead. Cordero slowed, trying to judge his next move.

The grille behind him exploded. The tyrannosaurus's snout smashed through. It shook its head, snorting in frustration, straining to reach Cordero. Defeated, it withdrew.

Before he could move, it burst through the grille right next to him.

Cordero rolled aside, onto his belly. He righted himself, scrambling away from the wall.

Booming footsteps passed overhead. He heard a deep snuffling. Another grille exploded a few feet ahead of him.

He couldn't keep this up. The tyrannosaurus would persist until it had him cornered. Even if he managed to escape the room, it wouldn't give up. It had his scent now.

There was no use running, he realized. He had to turn and fight.

He scrambled towards the closest wall. The thunder of footsteps told him that the tyrannosaurus was following. Looking up, he saw one of the heating pipes nearby. Partway up was a pressure release valve.

Perfect.

Before the tyrannosaurus could get any closer, Cordero leapt directly upwards. The grille above him spun away, clattering against the floor several feet away. The tyrannosaurus turned to face it, following the sound.

Cordero unhooked the shock stick from his harness. He raised it above his head, then swung it down as hard as he could.

The stick slammed into the valve, which tore loose, releasing a cloud of blistering steam that Cordero barely dodged. The tyrannosaurus, distracted, was enveloped in the boiling hot spray. It staggered backwards, roaring in agony.

Cordero ran blindly. The steam cleared, and he realized that he was back in the Nexus Chamber. This was bad; it was too close to Shea.

She was still at the console. "I need more time!" she shouted.

He looked around wildly, wondering what to do next. The tyrannosaurus would be on them in moments.

There was a sign on the wall alongside him. *Storeroom*. That was no use. Then, beneath it, *Cryogenics*.

An idea formed in Cordero's mind.

The tyrannosaurus roared from the storeroom. It was emerging from the steam, coming towards him.

This time, Cordero ran towards it, into the storeroom. The tyrannosaurus lunged, jaws wide. Cordero ducked to the side, feeling razor fangs brush against the fabric of his suit.

The tyrannosaurus swung its head towards him. It hit Cordero with the force of a truck, sending him flying.

This is gonna hurt.

His shoulder took the brunt of it, crunching with the impact. He rolled, thankful for all the low opening training that Recon had put him through.

He bounded out of the roll into a sprint. The thunder of the footsteps behind him gave him wings. He ran straight for the crane.

There was a ladder on the inside of the frame, going up to the control cabin. As he passed another pipe, he hit the valve with the shock stick. He was rewarded with another spray of steam.

Thankful for the momentary cover, he ducked inside the frame. The ladder rattled nauseatingly as he climbed.

At first, he thought that it was loose, then he realized the entire crane was swaying.

The tyrannosaurus emerged from the cloud of steam. Patches of its purple skin were blistered and raw, and one of its eyes was a milky white.

Cordero climbed faster.

The tyrannosaurus leapt. Its jaws slammed shut on the frame around Cordero. He stared in horror down into its cavernous throat, gagging on its rank breath.

The frame creaked, bending under the pressure of the beast's jaws.

Cordero jabbed the shock stick through the frame into the tyrannosaurus's tongue. He squeezed the trigger.

The monster roared, releasing the frame, and fell away.

The crane swayed crazily. Cordero wrapped his arms around the ladder. The frame was twisted and bent; it looked unlikely to survive another assault.

Cordero continued to climb. He had no other choice.

His shoulder screamed with each rung. The climb felt like it took him hours. Lifting his arms over his head was a titanic effort. Something was dislocated, or possibly worse. He gritted his teeth and breathed through the pain.

Finally, mercifully, he pulled himself onto the small platform at the top of the crane. He dragged himself to his feet and surveyed the room below.

The store was hot and humid, full of steam from the broken pipes. Through the mist, he could see the top of the shipping crates. The entrance to the cryogenics chamber was just beyond those, he recalled.

The crane shook violently, knocking Cordero to the floor. He landed hard, the shock stick falling, knocked from his grasp. It rolled towards the edge of the platform.

No!

Cordero lunged, just as the crane tilted wildly to one side. The stick bounced upwards, towards the edge. He stretched a hand out towards it.

It sailed over the edge.

Right into his hand.

Cordero gripped the mesh platform with his other hand, just as he flew over the edge. He jolted to a stop, the skin of his fingers tearing as he strained to support his entire body weight.

He hung by one hand from the tilting crane. Desperate, he swung from side to side in an attempt to leverage himself back onto the platform.

There was a growl from below.

The crane shook violently. Cordero nearly lost his grip. Blood poured down his arm from his shredded fingers.

The platform suddenly dropped before jolting to a stop.

Cordero looked down. The tyrannosaurus was directly beneath him, worrying at the gantry with its jaws. Its broad back was directly beneath his feet.

There was only one thing to do.

He let go.

He landed hard on the dinosaur's back, at the base of its neck. The tyrannosaurus tossed its head back, trying to reach him.

Digging his bloodied fingers into its scarred hide, Cordero swung a leg over its spine. He dragged himself forwards, avoiding the snapping jaws, until he was at the base of its skull. Unable to reach him, the tyrannosaurus began to buck like a bronco. It tossed its head from side to side, while slamming itself against the nearest wall.

Cordero gritted his teeth and clung on. His fingers were torn to shreds and his eardrums felt to have burst from the volume of the tyrannosaurus's angry roaring, but he refused to let go.

He waited until the beast tired and stopped for a moment, and jabbed the stun stick directly into the base of its skull.

"Time for a nap, Barney."

The tyrannosaurus screamed. It was a strange sound; a high-pitched yelp of pain, and anger at becoming the prey. The shock stick must have been damaged, as the safety regulator did not activate, allowing thousands of bolts to flow straight into the dinosaur's nervous system.

The monster lurched forwards, limbs spasming. It shook its head, desperate to escape the stabbing agony in its skull.

Blinded, it staggered towards the cryogenics chamber. Partway there, it stumbled, veering to the left and away from the door.

Cordero dug the head of the shock stick into its left temple.

The beast bellowed and flinched to the right, twisting away from the fiery torment. Cordero jabbed it again, and again, over, and over.

The tyrannosaurus staggered, then began to fall. Cordero jumped from its back, landing hard. He spun to face the creature.

The tyrannosaurus landed onto its side, half inside the cryogenic chamber. It thrashed its powerful legs blindly. Cordero leapt back. He kept away a distance, waiting.

The lights were on in the chamber, he noticed. It still had power. That was something to be thankful for.

Icy mist coated the chamber floor. A thin frost clung to the door frame. Glancing past the tyrannosaurus's convulsions, Cordero spotted a control panel alongside the door.

The tyrannosaurus was recovering. It rolled over to right itself, and rolled back into the storeroom.

Cordero sprinted at it, the shock stick raised over his head like a spear.

The monster spotted him with its good eye. It turned its head towards him and growled a bitter rumble of pure hatred, still struggling to stand.

Cordero yelled a wordless battle cry. He stabbed the stick deep into the tyrannosaurus's remaining eye.

With a harsh crack and a flash of blinding light, the shock stick exploded.

Cordero was thrown backwards, his arm numbed by the electrical discharge. He fell to the floor, his muscles shuddering.

The tyrannosaurus's legs gave out from under it. It dropped, collapsing through the doorway into the cryogenics chamber.

Cordero stood. His legs shook underneath him, and his shoulder still thundered with pain, but he didn't let anything slow him down. He rushed to the control panel and scoured it frantically.

"Come on, come on, where are..."

A furious roar came from within the midst of the cryogenic chamber. The tyrannosaurus was searching for him.

He scrolled through the system menus. *Maintenance mode. Partial Thaw. Full Thaw.* Where was it?

"Ha!" He punched the air, as a heavy footstep sounded from within the chamber.

Full Freeze.

"Welcome to the ice age, Barney!" he yelled, and slammed a fist down onto the icon.

The chamber door slammed shut. A fraction of a second later, something slammed against the far side, causing the door - and the wall around it - to shudder.

Cordero rushed to the viewing port.

At first, he could see nothing, just billowing clouds of mist that seemed to move of their own accord. He could feel the cold even through the thick door.

Then, he spotted a shadow. It was huge, crocodilian. The tyrannosaurus.

It waved its head from side to side, jaws wide. As Cordero watched, its movements started to slow.

Then, it stopped, slumped, and disappeared into the freezing mists.

TWENTY-THREE

Shea ran to Cordero and threw her arms around his shoulders. He winced audibly.

"Oh my god, I'm sorry," she said, releasing him and stepping back. She gasped when she saw the bruises on his face, and the unnatural way he held his arm. "Are you ok? What happened?"

"I got rid of the tyrannosaurus," he said simply. He tried to shrug, then winced as his shoulder flared with pain. "Didn't find the transformer though."

"Don't worry." Shea patted the console. "I snuck into the store while you drew out the rex. Took me a bit of searching but I found one."

"So we're ready to go?"

Shea looked pensive. "I've made the changes that're needed and I've inputted the commands. Theoretically, we should be able to step through then turn around and step right back onto Earth."

"Theoretically?"

"There are some... vagaries around the timings," she said. "The principle is that, once our mass passes through the portal, the Nexus will change direction. Direction as in its space-time location, you understand."

"Not really, but go on." Cordero leaned against the railing, rubbing his shoulder.

"I know that I can get us through, but I don't know how long it will take for the portal to switch back."

She was being vague. Deliberately so, he suspected. "So, once we pass through, we will have to wait until it's safe to come back through?"

"Basically."

"How long will we have to wait?"

She shook her head. "It's impossible to tell. Could be a few seconds. Could be, well, years."

"Years?" Cordero almost shouted, then caught himself. The last thing they needed was to attract the attention of some other hungry monster. *"Years,"* he hissed. "In the Cretaceous?"

"It's a gamble," she said. "But it's the only chance we have."

"I hate to gamble," Cordero grumbled. He straightened and turned to face the portal. It shimmered, like oil on water. There were shapes moving on the far side, though what they were he couldn't tell. It looked like the surface of the sea. With sharks lurking beneath. "How will we know when it's safe to try?"

"I've worked something out for that." She picked up a tablet from the console. "I've programmed this to read the particle flow of the portal. Once it registers the flow has changed, it will let us know."

"So," he said. "We step through, and we wait."

She nodded. "And hope."

They walked up to the portal together. It loomed over them, casting an eerie purple light over them, the entrance to another world. To Hell, Cordero thought.

Cordero felt Shea's hand on his. He looked down at it, then up at her face.

"Are you ready?" he asked.

She swallowed, nodded.

He took a breath. Held it. Then stepped forward.

One moment, he was on the *Buckland*, in the cool conditioned air of the Nexus Chamber. The next, he was bathed in heat. The air was thick, soupy, and stank of rotting vegetation. Cordero stepped forwards, sand crunching beneath his boots.

They stood on a shallow hill, dotted with stubby shrubs. To the south, the wasteland gave way to a murky lake surrounded by a copse of tall, tropical trees. A jagged mountain range on the horizon belched smoke and ash into the ruddy red sky.

A deep roar reverberated through the air. A pack of chicken-sized lizards - Cordero had no idea what breed of dinosaur they were - scattered from the shadows of the trees, squawking in terror.

"How's that portal looking?" he asked, eyes never leaving the tree line.

"Nothing so far." The frantic tapping of Shea's fingers on the tablet screen sounded incongruous in this place.

The roar came again. He couldn't be sure, but it sounded closer. Unthinking, his hand went to his hip for a pistol that was no longer there.

The ground beneath Cordero's feet began to vibrate with sudden, rhythmic shudders. He looked around for a weapon; a rock, a stick, anything, but couldn't find anything suitable. They were defenseless.

"Still nothing," Shea said before he could ask, her voice tight with fear.

The vibrations got stronger. They sounded to be getting closer. The sound of snapping wood came from amongst the trees.

"We need to go, now," Cordero said. "Even if it's back to the *Buckland.*"

"We can't." He turned to look at her. Her eyes were wide. "Look."

His gaze followed hers back to the portal. It still shimmered, but the color had changed. The purple glow was gone, replaced with a solid silver, like a pool of liquid mercury.

"The transition has commenced," Shea explained. "Once we stepped through, the process started. It can't be stopped, not now. And until it finishes, we're stuck here."

A loud splintering sound got their attention. They turned back to face the copse of trees.

The top of a fallen tree could be seen sticking out from within the shadows of the others. As they watched, another tree fell, crashing to the ground in a cloud of dust.

The head of a tyrannosaurus emerged from the trees. Its beady eyes fixed on Cordero and Shea immediately.

The tyrannosaurus stepped out into the harsh sunlight. It was enormous, even larger than the beast on the *Buckland* had been. Its jaws hung open, revealing jagged teeth dripping in thick coils of drool. Its thick hide was patterned with hundreds of scars, mementos of past battles.

The tyrannosaurus roared and advanced towards them.

Cordero backed away, standing between Shea and the monster. If he was going to die, he was going down fighting.

"I'm sorry, Cordero," she said from being him.

"Mike," he said. "Call me Mike."

The tyrannosaurus got closer. Cordero could smell its rank, rotten odor, like carrion. He could see hundreds of insects buzzing around its bloody jaws.

Something bleeped behind him. Shea let out a squeal of relief.

"It's green, Mike. We need to go, *now!*"

Cordero spun and grabbed Shea around the waist, lifting her off the ground. He took a deep breath and stepped through the portal.

The last thing he heard was a furious roar.

TWENTY-FOUR

It was still hot. It was still humid.

Cordero collapsed to his knees, suddenly exhausted. He exhaled heavily, then took a deep, juddering breath. The hot air scorched his throat and lungs.

They were somewhere else, but he had no idea where. Or when.

Shea lay in the dirt beside him. As he watched, she dragged herself up into a sitting position and looked around.

"It's gone," she said finally.

"What?"

"The portal."

She was right. The shimmering doorway had vanished. They were alone on another low hill, this time surrounded by desert.

"We did it, Mike. We got through."

"We did." He couldn't argue with that. "But where are we?"

"Somewhere better than we were," she said. Then she began to laugh.

He smiled. He couldn't help it. It felt like a lifetime since he had heard a genuine laugh.

Shea sounded relieved. Her whole demeanor changed; the tension that he suddenly realized she'd been carrying around the entire time he'd known her had gone. Watching her, he felt calmer, he felt relief.

For the first time in a long time, he felt safe.

Cordero started to laugh too, in great, coughing guffaws. This made Shea laugh even harder, which had the same effect on him.

For a while, they just laughed together, enjoying the moment. Then they got quiet. Cordero noticed that Shea was staring at the sky.

"What is it?" he asked after a while.

She pointed.

He looked. There, in the pale blue sky, a pair of white lines of vapor, too straight to be natural.

"Contrails," he said, and a mundane word had never held such feeling for him. Despite the pain and the exhaustion, he had never felt better.

They were back.

THE END

Made in the USA
Monee, IL
30 March 2021

64415635R00085